Astro Saga

The Celestial Secrets

*The Second Secret, Second edition 2023,
Published by Oblique Media Group Ltd.
ISBN: 9781549926549*

Other books by Robert Smithbury also published by Oblique Media
www.oblique.media

ASTRO SAGA

The Celestial Secrets

Already published

The First Secret
The Third Secret
The Fourth Secret
The Fifth Secret
The Sixth Secret
The Seventh and Final Secrets

Faerielandz

Yet to be scheduled for publication

The Hamster, the Explorers and the Fridge

Princess De Stiny

The Vision of the Dawn Together

The Lost Battle

Further **Astro Saga** *adventures for future release*

The Earth Series

Torr Naydo and the King of Earth
Torr Naydo and the Battle for Earth

The Casebook of Armitage Shanks

The Mysterious case of Un-Life

The Voyages of the Spaceship Oceanius

Underworld
Colony and Conflict

Kezin: Bio-Gene Agent

Kezin in deep
Kezin's Pride
Kezin, Dragon Lord

The Second Secret

by

Robert Smithbury

ROBERT SMITHBURY
email: astro.saga.oblique.media@gmail.com

To Catherine, without whose support

I would never have got around to telling these stories

Contents

Living in an asteroid 9
Chapter 1: There's something following us 23
Chapter 2: Hiding in the freezer 35
Chapter 3: The Weird Circus of Dr Wonderfoul 43
Chapter 4: Kezin 57
Chapter 5: In the cage 65
Chapter 6: Attack of the Overnight bag 75
Chapter 7: Dr Wonderfoul's last words 85
Chapter 8: It's not as if it's a tail 99
Chapter 9: Into the worst blizzard ~ ever! 109
Chapter 10: Breakfast? 125
Chapter 11: The violent Verminx 137
Chapter 12: Caverns of Ice 145
Chapter 13: Hanging about... for a bit 157
Chapter 14: Into the pit 167
Chapter 15: Waterfall wars 177
Chapter 16: It's in the bag 187
Chapter 17: ...or is it? 197
Chapter 18: The Mysterious Mystery of the Fish 209

ROBERT SMITHBURY
email: astro.saga.oblique.media@gmail.com

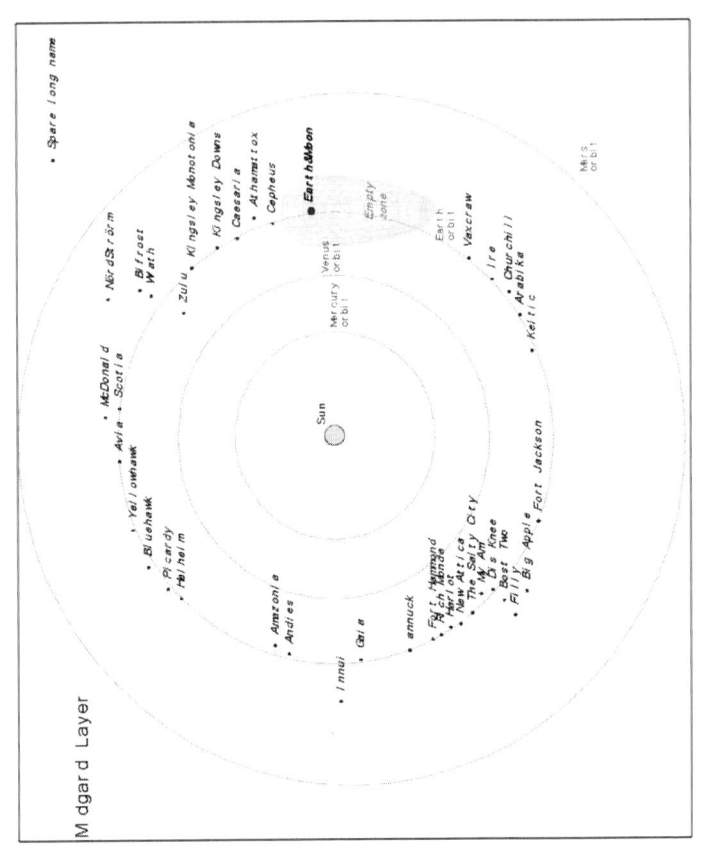

Map of the inhabited asteroids in earth orbit

This is a map of the 'Midgard' layer of Asteroids, which lies in rough alignment with the earth equator. The Midgard layer is the central layer of five layers of asteroids that were moved into earth orbit to provide additional living space for humanity.

Living in an asteroid

Following a cataclysm several centuries ago humanity has abandoned earth, compelled to find somewhere else to live to escape extinction.

The other planets around our sun are inhospitable places. Mankind needed to establish new homes that were about the same distance from the sun as the Earth. A place with space was needed for everyone. No one was to be left behind.

Asteroids are big, or at least some of them are. But not so massive that they can't be towed. Some of the larger asteroids were moved from the asteroid belt (between Mars and Jupiter) and placed into five orbits, tiered like the layers of a cake. Each orbit was roughly the same size and shape as the Earth's.

By hollowing out the interior of each asteroid and starting them spinning, humans created artificial habitats where they now live and occasionally thrive.

ROBERT SMITHBURY
email: astro.saga.oblique.media@gmail.com

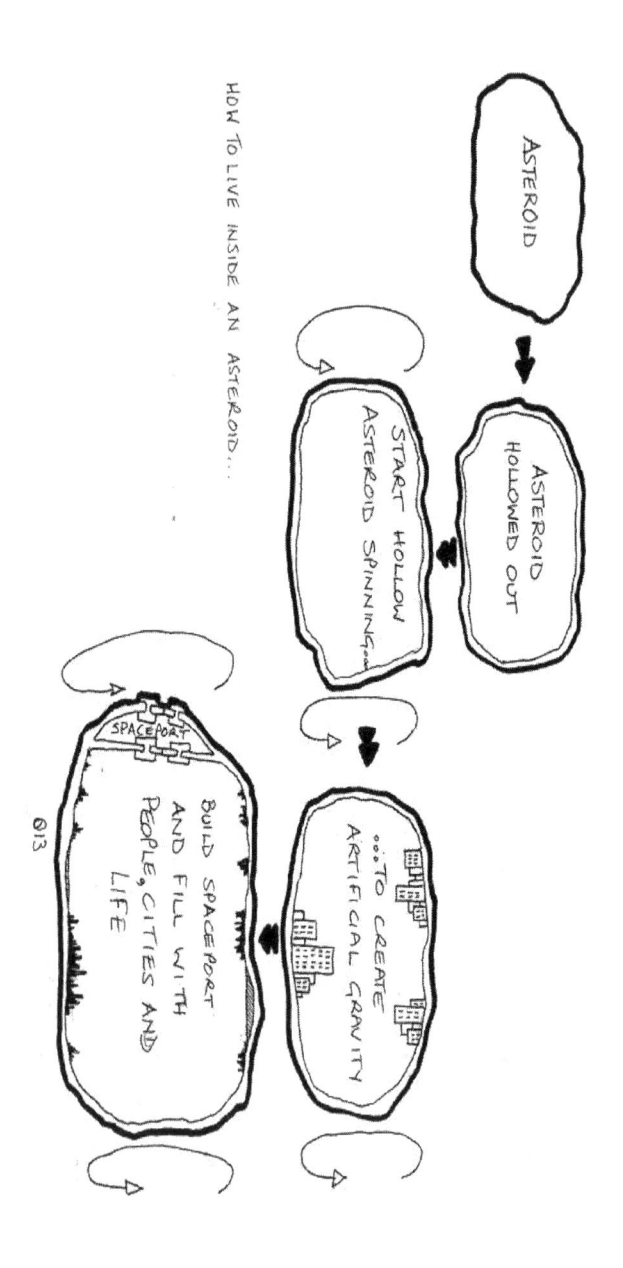

HOW TO LIVE INSIDE AN ASTEROID...

ASTEROID

↓

ASTEROID HOLLOWED OUT

→ START HOLLOW ASTEROID SPINNING...

↓

...TO CREATE ARTIFICIAL GRAVITY

→ BUILD SPACEPORT AND FILL WITH PEOPLE, CITIES AND LIFE

013

Prologue: Winter Wonderland

Two sinister, dark, hungry eyes watched the snowball hurtle through the air. It curved across the sky and out of sight before finally catching Sarah Sinclair on the side of her head. Ice crystals slipped under her collar and down her neck. She shivered and screamed in the way that only young girls can.

Ears flattened at the sharpness of the sound. Changing direction, a hunter's nose sniffed the air and caught the scent; small humans, hmmm.

"I'll get you for that, Jason!" Sarah's thin voice trilled in the chilling winter's air. It gave a clear direction to the hidden hunter.

Ursine synapses pondered. Sensitive nostrils scented warm meat, still fresh. Definitely somewhere near. Taste buds salivated. A thick, blue tongue licked hairy, frosted lips surrounding strong, sharp fangs.

Sarah shook the melting ice from her hair and bent low to gather up handfuls of snow, forging them into a frozen ball of unpleasantness for her brother. Vengeance called.

Hunger gnawed, hunger urged, hunger growled, unwittingly interrupting the silence of the freshly fallen snowfield.

Sarah turned at the unexpected noise. "What was that?"

Hunger forced a painful hush.

Silence, once more.

"Jason, was that you?"

Slow breaths, steamed in the cold air. Paws pressed down on the thick covering of fresh snow, searching for a solid grip on the hard ground beneath. Claws gripped, tense, expectant. Perhaps a step further forwards? Movement slowed, time stretched.

"Jason?" Sarah hissed and whispered slowly, urgently, pleadingly, quietly wishing.

In the sudden darkness that edged her vision it felt to her like the tendrils of the surrounding trees reached ominously out towards her, clutching anxiously at her coat.

The sound of a breaking twig shot the silence. Sarah leapt and ran, slipped and fell, all in one movement. Heavy breath lurched into the periphery of her vision, a searching shadow heading unerringly her way. A cold blade of twilight slipped into her soul. She tried to raise her head to find some clue, some inclination of what was happening, to no avail.

A sudden heavy weight crashed into her, knocking the last urgent, panting breath from her lungs, forcing her back down, leaping on top of her. She gasped to breathe. Another snowball was rubbed into her face, filling her mouth with slushy ice and leaves.

She tried to cry out but couldn't speak, "Spplttz!" was all that she could manage.

Sitting astride her, Jason was exultant. Oblivious to the hidden watcher, he gouged fresh handfuls of snow from the ground with his frozen fingers and rubbed them into his sister's hair with glee.

At the sound of triumphant laughter, muscles tensed, adrenaline surged, reflexes accelerated. Talons extended. Time slowed to a crawl. Hunter's eyes narrowed and focused, all senses converged on a single thought: food.

From his position of temporary triumph, prehistoric senses deep within Jason's brain flared and fought for his attention. Subconscious neural triggers vainly tried to warn him about the expectant hunter.

Satisfied that his sister was safely vanquished as she sobbed into the frozen ground beneath him, he glanced around warily. The wind howled around the two children, constantly shifting wooded shapes and shadows uncertainly.

Jason's skin crawled with mischievous, malicious imagination, urging him to heap further humiliation on his sister but something was stopping him. A new unknown fear appeared to be circling him just out of his vision. His thoughts filled with hesitation and uncertainty.

Even to his young, hesitant observations, the small wood had changed beyond recognition in the last few days. The last time he had left the house in the sharp, brightness of midsummer the trees had been a welcoming haven. Now, in the half gloom, they creaked with the unexpected weight of snow and cast long shadows in the limited, thinning daylight.

On the other side of the nearby hill his mother, Janx, scraped at the ice on the inside of the strengthened glass to get a better look at what was happening outside. Pensively she worried about what potential catastrophe might threaten them next.

Life had gone downhill for the whole family rapidly ever since the Solergy energy batteries had failed without warning only a few days ago. Immediately, all of NördStrörm's thermal systems had automatically cut their output by 90% to conserve energy. Normally, by preference, the weather in NördStrörm was kept mild verging on chilly. But now, with power at a premium, the asteroid engineers had reviewed the situation and reluctantly cut the thermal power further, shunting everyone straight into the middle of the deepest arctic winter ever known.

With no molten planetary core to call on for heat reserves, the extreme cold of deep space had quickly sucked any remaining warmth from the inhabited interior of the asteroid. An immense blizzard had hit in what should have been midsummer and a new ice age had started overnight. Rivers glaciated and fresh, sudden snow fell in sheets that blanketed the rapidly freezing ground. Frozen chaos fractured civilisation as it skidded to a halt, an ice road juggernaut caught in a 360-degree whiteout.

The sudden onslaught of the coldest weather Janx had ever known had rapidly depleted their cabin's energy reserves, as night was significantly extended by the government in an attempt to conserve further energy. In the subdued lighting of a new dawn she had come to the painful realisation of how reliant they were on the tiny energy cells, even with their tiny energy needs inside their pitifully tiny residence.

Without energy to generate heat the temperature in their small dwelling had dropped dramatically. Then the weather had taken another turn for the worse.

As a second chilling night fell the normal weather systems had ruptured and an intense storm had spread deep snow down from the mountains and buried the wood near their small home. Animals fled for heat preserving burrows. Roots ruptured in the frozen dirt.

Fortunately, the freak blizzard had blown itself out by the morning as weather systems struggled to re-stabilise around the unendurable arctic climate. In the dim half-life of an unnaturally foreshortened day, the children's excitement at the heavy snowfall had been easy to release. Janx had encouraged them to go out and play whilst she stayed indoors trying to figure out how to survive the days that lay ahead. Now she was beginning to regret letting them out of her sight. If only she could see what they were up to…

Jason stared frantically around him trying to quieten the surging sense of peril that was rapidly building up inside him. Fallen snow from overloaded boughs lay piled around in newly blown mounds. The one in front of him shifted and extended a nose, a mouth, a claw, another…

Jason didn't wait to see more of the hunter as it burst into the clearing. But to his credit he stopped long enough in his headlong flight to drag his sister and scream at her to run for her life.

With its quarry in full flight, the enormous polar bear accelerated at an amazing pace for its three metre long frame. This was a game it knew how to win. Huge lungs pumped oxygen to muscles that burnt energy at a furious pace in the hunter's race with its chosen prey. A colourless blur on white, a surging tide of furry snow, an avalanche of awesome ferocity, it descended upon the fleeing children.

Free of the wood and its restraining trees the hunter's quarry burst into the open, rushing across the frozen lawn towards the distant log cabin. Its welcoming wisp of smoke trailed into the sky, beckoning with a gossamer thin hope of sanctuary. Jason prayed he'd see the inside again.

"Mummy!" screamed Sarah.

"Save your breath for running," panted Jason alongside her, wasting his own.

Above the roar of his own heart thumping in his ears he could sense the thundering footfalls of the giant polar bear relentlessly gaining on him. From some hidden reserve Sarah found a new source of energy and she began to move ahead of Jason, her longer legs opening up a life saving gap.

Closer, closer, nearly there, keep going. Wear them down. Rip their hides. Snap their bones. Tear their meat. Taste their screams. Rend their dreams.

From inside the cabin Janx heard the screaming and rushed back to the window in alarm as her fears manifested, chilling her heart as solid as the water in the brutally broken, fatally fractured pipes.

Her eyes frantically scanned the white hillside for signs of imminent jeopardy. Apart from the screams there were none. Across the snow covered meadow she could see the children rushing towards her, voices loud but indistinct. There was nothing else to indicate any apparent danger. Perhaps they had only been screams of laughter, she thought, prematurely quietening her concerns.

Suddenly, her illusory complacency splintered, shattering into slithers of fear as the huge bear crested the hill and cannoned along in pursuit of her children. It rapidly gained on them as they hurtled down the slope. A primeval scream ripped its way clear of her throat as she ran towards the door with vain, faint hopes of rescue and self-sacrifice.

Finding himself between the giant, hunter, killer bear and his sister, Jason lengthened his stride as the heavy, wooden cabin door opened ahead of him. Several steps later Sarah threw herself through the gap and from somewhere much too close behind him, the bear roared and prepared to leap across the remaining distance between it and its prey.

Whether it was a roar of frustration, or triumph, Jason didn't wait to find out and launched himself towards possible salvation. His only chance of survival remained in crossing the threshold before the bear's claws could impale him. As he passed through the welcome opening he landed atop his sister for a second time that day. Together they scrambled for cover. Behind them Janx slammed the door shut and jammed down the hefty cross bars.

She prayed that the wood would hold against the giant bear's thunderous assault.

There was a rending, explosive crash as the hunter collided with the sudden and unexpected barrier that was preventing it reaching its prey. The whole cabin juddered to its foundations as the bear's onslaught threatened to demolish the whole, suddenly fragile, construct in its rage.

Then silence. They listened to their hearts beat wildly as wide-eyed they panted with exhaustion on the cold, unforgiving floor.

One.

Two.

Three.

Then a bellow of rage as the cabin shuddered again under a fresh onslaught. Cracks began to appear in the door's weaker beams as the bear assaulted their refuge, hammering on the walls with furious fists, splintering wood with swipes of its carnassial claws.

Jason and Sarah fled, scampering into the next room and straight underneath the beds as their mother hastened to shutter the remaining windows before joining them. Crawling into the slim, dark, space they crushed their squeezing, wheezing tears and fears tightly together.

"We should be safe here," Janx whispered, hoping that her words were more likely to come true than their chances of surviving through this unexpected winter. If that giant bear managed to get in she didn't want to think about what it could do.

No, what it would surely do

ROBERT SMITHBURY
email: astro.saga.oblique.media@gmail.com

Chapter 1: There's something following us...

Torr awoke in shock at the screaming sound in the cabin and as he opened his eyes the flashing overhead lights overloaded his eyes. For a moment he couldn't remember where he was and then reality came crashing in. He was aboard the Eos, in search of the Second Celestial Secret, supposedly donated by aliens, stolen by two evil empires and desperately needed by all humanity. Somewhere along the way he was hoping to locate his lost parents.

In the last few weeks his average, normal, life had become a lot more complicated.

Nattie burst into his room and shouted noiselessly in an effort to be heard. He could see her lips moving but couldn't make out the words above the deafening klaxon.

A small voice inside his head was trying to make itself heard. To make matters worse, Fuzz ball rolled into the room and started running around it in broken circles. Lights flashed in neon colours and pandemonium truly reigned.

"KIKI! MAKE IT STOP!" Torr shouted at the top of his voice.

The noise ceased as suddenly as it had started and only its echoes remained, leaping around inside Torr's skull. In shock, Fuzz ball ran into the table, bounced helplessly before missing her balance and falling to the floor.

"What was all that about?" Nattie asked, carefully removing her hands from her ears in case there was any sudden resurgence of noise.

Torr held his aching head in his hands, "Kiki? Care to explain? Quietly though!" he emphasised.

"Sure boss. Oh, and I forgot to say 'Good Morning'. Good morning," Kiki sang in a syrupy, cheerful voice.

"Good morning Kiki," Nattie whispered, wearing a faint, crooked smile. She couldn't help but feel amused.

The lights of the room faded back into a soft glow. Between Torr's feet, the overnight bag crept out gingerly from underneath the bed with both handles wrapped firmly across its zip. It looked clearly annoyed.

Torr was unwilling to forgive Kiki so easily and waved an irritated hand in the air.

"Get on with it," he growled.

"I think there might be someone following us," said Kiki.

The Tinkerer had claimed that Kiki, the onboard computer, had a child friendly personality overlay, but Torr had his doubts. He couldn't find anything particularly child friendly about the way that Kiki behaved.

"Someone's following us?" Torr asked, silently dreading the answer.

"Someone's following us," Kiki chirped cheerfully.

"Who?"

"I don't know. If I knew that I'd have said."

"So how do you know that we're being followed then?"

"Because every time we change course, they change course in exactly the same way and keep coming directly for us. In my book that counts as being followed. How do you define it?"

Torr ignored the question and instead glanced across at Nattie. She looked scared. Her smile had totally vanished. Fuzz ball scratched at her head and took Nattie's hand between her large soft paws as her fur wafted in waves.

"You don't think it's the Nebulon III do you?" Nattie asked nervously. Her recent incarceration on the Typhon had made her naturally cautious about evil empires and their dark designs.

"Kiki?" Torr asked, reluctantly knowing that he needed the computer's assistance.

"It doesn't look like the Nebulon III," the computer answered huffily. "I think I would recognise the biggest battleship in the Carthaginian fleet."

He sounded like his feelings were hurt.

"You mean you can see it?" Torr leapt from the bed. It always amazed him how Kiki could hide important pieces of information in plain sight.

"Sure."

"Why didn't you tell me?! Don't answer that. I know the answer, because I didn't ask you. Just show us now, OK."

Torr talked rapidly to avoid Kiki getting a word in. But nevertheless Kiki managed to give the impression of sullen, reluctant acceptance that the game was over, without making a single sound.

They all rushed into the main cabin where the large viewing screen was brightening. As they watched with growing anxiety, an object with long rotating wings and a worrying array of weapons slid towards them. It was gliding carefully between the multitude of spinning asteroids and floating remnants of a failed construction boom. Unerringly it kept all of the missiles pointing at them through every twist and turn it made.

Torn between watching the lethally equipped drone and the huge revolving rocks that spiralled silently in space, Torr wondered whether the people living inside them knew that heavily armed death was passing so closely by their door. He felt sure that their community safety computers hadn't woken them loudly with worrying tales of alarm and concern.

"Ugly, armed and dangerous," muttered Nattie, biting her lip.

"Perhaps we should take the Eos up into another layer," suggested Torr, "maybe the Behomian layer. We might give it the slip that way."

"Probably not. It's pretty persistent." replied Kiki. "Tracker drones usually are."

"What's the Behomian layer?" asked Nattie. It wasn't a phrase she had heard before.

"All of the asteroids in Earth's orbit are arranged in five layers," explained Torr as if he were some form of expert. "Kingsley Downs, where we found the First Celestial Secret, is in the Midgard layer, which roughly equates with the equator on earth. The layer 'north', or 'above', of Midgard is the Behomian layer."

Torr could see Nattie's eyes glazing over. He wasn't making it very clear and tried again.

"Think of it as a jam sponge cake. Some asteroids orbit in the jam layer in the middle and some orbit in either the upper or lower bits of sponge. No asteroid moves between the layers."

Fuzz ball's eyes also glazed and her vivid imagination turned inwards at all of this talk of cake. Nattie was amusing herself by wondering how much of a mess would be made if the asteroids really did travel through giant layers of Victoria sponge.

"Is NördStrörm covered in jam or sponge then?" she asked in her best and most innocent voice, goading him with assumed ignorance.

But as Nattie asked her supposedly harmless question about their destination, Torr felt a shiver go down his spine and a hole open up in his stomach at the merest thought of jam sponge cake. NördStrörm;

the very name frightened him. With that in front of him and the heavily armed tracker drone behind, he felt trapped between an unavoidably hideous destiny and an unrelentingly deadly pursuer.

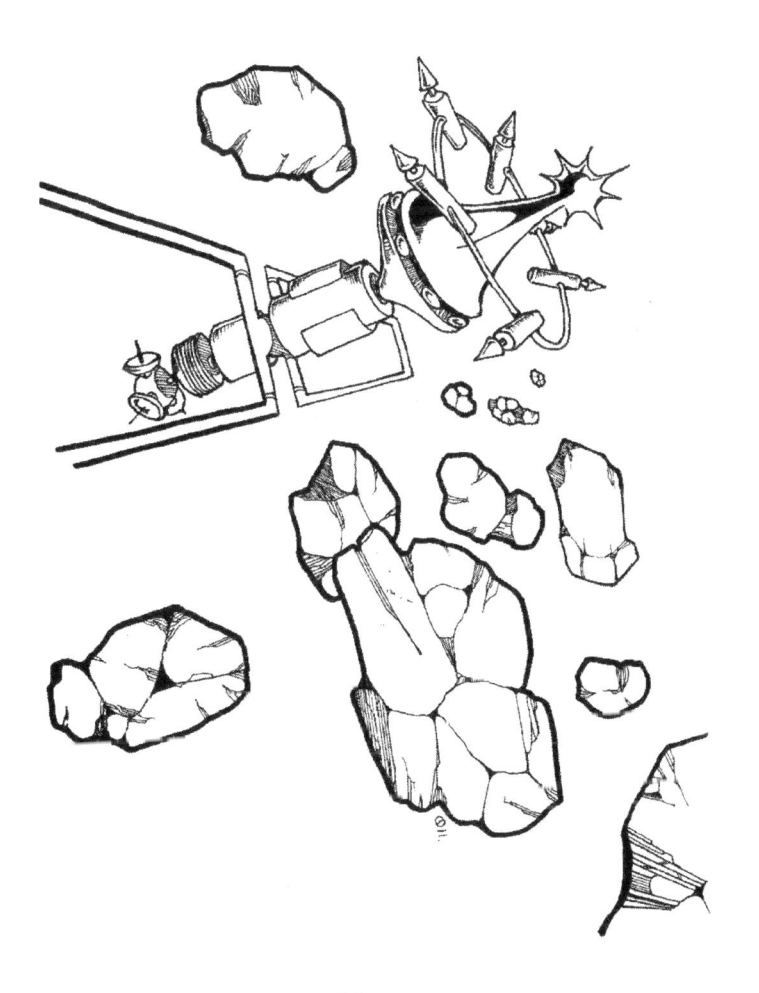

"How is that thing following us?" Torr muttered, half to himself. "Space is crowded this near to Earth. There should be no way it can keep track of us amongst the millions of objects out here."

"That's easy", chirped Kiki. "It's a tracker drone and it's following our Automatic Navigation Pilot signal."

"You mean our ANP is on?" Torr asked in disbelief.

He and Nattie stared at each other in disbelief. Some days computers could be so stupid. They shouted in unison, "SHUT IT OFF!"

"Okey, dokey" replied Kiki, apparently oblivious to the tension that he was creating as he blithely switched off the very technology they had worked so hard to recover on Kingsley Downs.

Silently they stared at each other holding their breath.

"Well?" whispered Torr.

For a few seconds there was only the hum of the engines being engaged before the computer spoke again.

"I've tried a couple of simple manoeuvres without any corresponding movement from the tracking drone, so that seems to have worked."

They all relaxed visibly.

"But it's now trying a search pattern. It knows it's lost us and has started looking more thoroughly. Tracker drones are known for their persistence."

Torr was thinking furiously, "We can't afford the fuel to take too much evasive action. Now that the Aztex have most probably started tampering with the Second Celestial Secret they've disrupted its technology and as a result the Solergy energy cells have stopped working. That's severely affected how much energy we have available, which means we're on reserve power batteries and we've only just got enough fuel left to get us to NördStrörm. We can't dodge around too much whilst trying to lose the tracker drone."

Another shiver quivered down his backbone and settled with the others hiding in his stomach. It neatly filled the hole left behind by his thoughts of jam sponge cake. A proper breakfast would have helped his digestion better. His Uncle Otto had been right; a good breakfast is very important. Especially if you're trying to pull one over on an evil empire, thought Torr.

"And with everyone else conserving fuel as well, if we tried too hard to escape by jetting away quickly then we'd show up like a sore thumb for acting so differently," added Nattie.

The overnight bag crawled back underneath the bed and started shivering and shaking. It had a sensitive constitution and wasn't really built for the worries of long distance travelling. Watching it shuffle awkwardly into the darkness gave Nattie an idea.

"We could hide!" she exclaimed, slightly too loudly for Torr's ears which were still ringing from the alarms that had started his day.

"Where?" he asked quietly.

"I don't know. Kiki, any ideas?" Nattie asked.

"Hmmmm," hummed Kiki helpfully. "Hmmmm."

"That's all I need," muttered Torr darkly, "an indecisive computer."

"Humph!" said Kiki. "Well, I had thought of somewhere to hide. But I'm not going to tell you if you are going to be insulting. You'll have to figure it out by yourself," he finished defiantly.

"Kiki!" Torr and Nattie shouted at the walls together. Even Fuzz ball went over and kicked the control console. She regretted it instantly and hopped around the room, holding one foot between her paws, before falling over onto her back.

The computer didn't respond, instead remaining eerily silent. This was so unusual that all of them felt unsettled.

"Kiki, if we don't evade this tracker drone, we're all going to die. You included. Didn't the Tinkerer programme any sense of self preservation into you?" Nattie asked, trying intellect where shouting had failed.

"Well," Kiki said with deliberate slowness. "There is this hollow asteroid a short distance away. It was excavated to provide living accommodation in the last construction boom but was never finished due to lack of funds. If we slipped inside it and turned off all of the power sources, then the tracker drone might not find us. We could then slip out again and continue on our way to NördStrörm. But I have to emphasise the word 'might'."

"Do it, before I take you apart screw by screw and transistor by transistor," Torr threatened.

Intellectual deviousness wasn't something he could consider on an empty stomach.

"It's going to get cold," Kiki warned in retaliation. He didn't like being shouted at.

"If we turn all of the power off that's going to include the heating. The temperature will drop quickly. Are you absolutely sure that's what you want to do?"

Nattie put her hand on Torr's shoulder in an attempt to prevent his temper overheating. She could feel the tension in his muscles.

"Just do it Kiki. Come on guys, time to put on all of our warm clothes and space suits."

She reached under the bed and grabbed the handles of the overnight bag, dragging it out into the open, "That means you too."

"I just hope this works and we don't freeze to death waiting for the tracker drone to forget about us," Torr muttered, biting his nails but following her lead.

No one appeared to be listening, they were all too busy struggling into heavy jumpers and extra pairs of socks.

No change there, he thought. No one ever seems to listen.

Chapter 2: Hiding in the freezer

With frost caking the inside of the windows they huddled together in near darkness. Kiki had hidden the Eos inside the hollow asteroid and turned off all of the power except for one tiny light. It was a desperate attempt to 'disappear' from any devices that the tracker drone might be using to try and find them. They could only sit and wait in the hope that their strategy would be effective.

"I feel so cold that I'm going numb," muttered Nattie. "There's no sensation in my toes."

"At least we're not using up any energy," Kiki joked. "We should still have enough to get us to NördStrörm."

"How did we get into this mess?" whispered Torr rhetorically. "I feel like I'm hiding in someone's freezer."

The cold was seeping deep into his bones and his teeth were chattering. Talking helped, a little.

"I mean, all we did was happen to come across an attack on a covert satellite and rescue a survivor. Then we tried to get him some help, which led us to the Tinkerer and before I know it he sends me off on some crazy mission to save mankind. Strangely it seemed like the right thing to do at the time."

Torr paused to think, "And besides, I'm not sure he's human! What sort of grown up would send a boy out to save humanity? Normally they'd be saying things like 'It's time for bed' and 'Haven't you got any homework to do?' Not the Tinkerer, 'Will you help me save all mankind?' he says. Sometimes I wonder why me? Why can't I just have a normal life like everybody else?"

"Oh, come on Torr," interrupted Nattie between shivers. "Much as that might sound very noble you know it's not all of the story. What about finding your parents? The Tinkerer promised you that if we could recover the Seven Celestial Secrets then he could probably use them to help you find your missing parents. We've got the first one. It's not much but it's a start." "Very convenient," said Torr, trying to ignore Fuzz ball's vigorous nodding and the way her fur swayed as she shivered. The whole effect was very distracting. "This whole thing with the alien technology and the fighting between the Aztex and Carthaginian Empires over it all - why did the aliens let the seven pieces of technology get stolen in the first place? If they're so clever..."

He stopped to watch Fuzz ball shake her head.

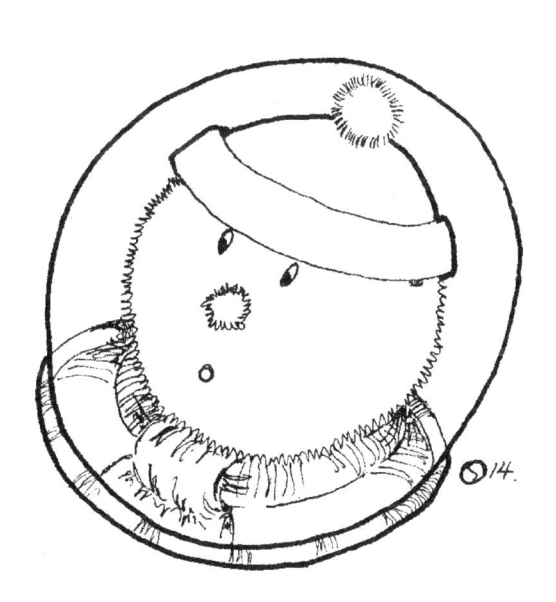

"And stop that! You're making me giddy."

The rising tension of sitting in a freezing space ship hoping they wouldn't be discovered was making him irritable.

Nattie dug him deliberately in the ribs, hard.

"Don't take it out on Fuzz ball. It's not her fault. We're all in this together. You know that more than anyone. You were one of the first people to be affected by the First Secret being opened, preventing all of the ANPs from working. If you hadn't sorted it out by recovering the First Celestial Secret and getting it to the Tinkerer so he could repair it, then a lot of people would be dead right now."

"Hmmmph!" muttered Torr grudgingly. He didn't like admitting she was right but he did enjoy it when she gave him all the credit for recovering the First Secret.

The truth was, he'd had some help.

"And now we need to sort out the Second Celestial Secret as well. If our energy batteries are only operating at 10% of their normal levels, then it's likely that the Aztex have tried to open the Second Celestial Secret as well, causing it to shut down everywhere. If we don't get it back and over to the Tinkerer so he can fix it then we're going to freeze to death and probably the rest of humanity won't be far behind us," Nattie said quickly, the words all coming out in a rush.

As she spoke she fiddled nervously with the handles of the overnight bag that had emerged again from beneath the bed. It had a satisfied look on its face as Nattie 'scratched' between its handles. Torr was sure he could hear it purring. A bag that purred made no sense but then the Eos was full of things made no sense and that he didn't, or couldn't, understand.

"Besides," she continued before Torr could interrupt. "We're the only ones who know that the Second Celestial Secret is on NördStrörm, because we're the only ones with a tracing device that tells us where they all. And so we're the only ones who can do anything about it. It's all up to us."

"Aha!" said Torr jumping up, pointing directly at Nattie. "The Tinkerer made the tracker and so he could know where it is as well. He could recover it."

"Yes, well," said Nattie, crossing her arms defiantly, which was an impressive act whilst wearing several layers of clothes and a space suit, "if we left it all to the Tinkerer to do, then who's going to lead the search for your parents?"

"Okay," said Torr, deflated by the obviousness of her logic. "There you may have a point." He sat down again heavily.

Nattie continued confidently, "And don't forget the Carthaginians in the Nebulon III. If they find the Celestial Secrets before we do, goodness knows what would happen."

"You're right," admitted Torr, feeling depressed again for entirely different reasons. It was all a bit too overwhelming. His head sunk into his hands. "I guess it's just a bit too frightening. Sometimes it all gets overwhelming. I feel like I'm drowning in it all."

Fuzz ball put her big furry arms around Torr and hugged him heavily. Nattie laughed.

"At least we have each other!" she giggled in an attempt to cheer him up before collapsing into another trembling shiver.

"Yeah, right," said Torr.

But that didn't stop him from hugging Fuzz ball back. It felt good cuddling Fuzz ball. He felt it was somehow reassuring snuggling up to a big, soft, round, furry... erm... thing.

"When Kiki was telling me about NördStrörm he was saying that apparently, it was populated by a group of people who wanted to live like Vikings so they turn the temperature way down across most of the asteroid to get great winters. In small pockets of warmth they have half-hearted summers but it never gets really warm. I can't imagine how cold it is now that everyone has a lot less energy to heat their homes with. They started off cold and now they must be freezing. They probably really need our help, right now," whispered Nattie.

Torr couldn't help but agree. NördStrörm was not only where the Second Celestial Secret was hidden but it was also somewhere that was badly affected by the effects of its chilling failure. Much as he didn't want to, he had to go to NördStrörm and recover the secret alien technology that would hopefully save mankind from the frigid terror of icy space.

Lots of lives were depending on him.

ROBERT SMITHBURY
email: astro.saga.oblique.media@gmail.com

Chapter 3: The Weird Circus of Dr Wonderfoul

Both Torr and Nattie breathed a frosty, collective sigh of relief when Kiki finally gave the all clear.

"I'm going to shut down a lot of the unnecessary systems and reduce power to others so that we conserve as much energy as possible," he added.

"Will it be warm?" asked Torr, who had already had enough of being cold.

"Slightly cooler than normal but you should be fine," answered Kiki. "You'll hardly notice it, or the reduced gravity."

"Reduced gravity?" said Torr, pushing Nattie gently away from him.

She slid backwards, her feet lifting slightly from the ground.

"Heh!"

Moments later the Eos re-emerged from the asteroid where it had been hidden, silent and surreptitious. Nattie smiled as she noticed how Fuzz ball had inter-twined herself with the overnight bag.

The two of them looked quite sweet, snuggled together. This reminded her of the unpalatable future that awaited them. It wasn't going to be as easy to recover the Second Celestial Secret as it had been to retrieve the first.

"Guess we ought to get on our way to NördStrörm," she said looking sideways at Torr, not sure about how he would react to her reminder.

"Yes, you're right," he replied, giving her a similar look before quickly averting his gaze. "Let's get this over with. Maybe then we might get a chance to get back to normality, although I'm beginning to forget what that feels like."

Nattie paused momentarily and touched his arm lightly, hesitantly. Torr looked back at her again. She looked indecisive and uncharacteristically unsure of herself.

"When we get to NördStrörm how are we going to find the Second Celestial Secret?" she asked him. "By now the Aztex will have removed it from their ship. It could be anywhere inside the asteroid."

Torr thought for a moment. She had a point.

"Perhaps we could get Kiki to set up a portable ANP tracker that we could carry along with us. You know, the way the Tinkerer fixed ours so we can track the Celestial Secrets across space. We could use it the same way inside the asteroid, but on a smaller scale." He turned to address the open air, "Kiki, would that be possible?"

The onboard speakers burst into life with that strange, over enthusiastic voice that Kiki thought children would find comforting. "Way ahead of you, Torr. I'm uploading a programme into my portable command module as we speak. It should enable us to do exactly what you've described."

"Well done, Kiki."

For a moment, to Torr, even the room lights looked brighter and more welcoming. He certainly felt more positive about their destination than he had earlier. Funny how just doing something, anything, made the future appear more attractive. He dared to allow himself a tiny smile, which evaporated as quickly as a snowflake on a summer's day.

"We have company," announced Kiki, shattering Torr's newfound sense of well being.

"What now?" sulked Torr, thrown abruptly back into a pit of despondency by the thought of having to hide in another asteroid. "It's not the tracker drone again is it?"

He slumped down into a nearby chair feeling deflated.

"No," replied Kiki. "It's another space ship. It's putting out a distress signal. They say they've run out of fuel and are stranded."

"Oh, for goodness' sake. I'm fed up with rescuing people," pouted Torr, irritability getting the better of him. "All we ever seem to do is rescue people. Zarrox, the Tinkerer, Nattie, and now this! When is someone going to rescue me?"

Nattie turned and confronted Torr where he sat, arms folded and shoulders hunched. She looked extremely annoyed.

"Well excuse me, I didn't actually need rescuing. Fuzz ball and I were doing very well rescuing ourselves if you don't mind. If we'd left it to you Fuzz ball would be dead now!"

Fuzz ball glared at Torr and slapped him across the leg. She remembered too clearly how Torr had placed her in mortal danger by not thinking through all of the consequences of his actions.

"Ow!" Torr glared at both of them. "Who is it anyway?" he asked, changing the subject to cover his own feelings of guilt.

"A circus," replied Kiki in a syrupy voice designed to calm the situation. It wasn't very effective. "Won't that be fun?"

"A circus?" Torr scowled. He didn't like circuses.

"A circus! How wonderful," giggled Nattie, clearly fascinated by the thought and desperate to lift Torr's mood. "Clowns, acrobats, maybe some performing animals."

"Don't you think it's cruel to keep animals trapped in cages, hauling them across space?" Torr growled.

He didn't like to think of anything being unfairly incarcerated.

"I couldn't bear being locked in a cage," shivered Nattie, her gaiety banished by Torr's question. "You have a point. It doesn't seem fair on them."

The plight of caged animals wasn't a perspective she had considered before. It was too close to her own experiences for comfort.

"I remember just being confined to that room on board the Typhon. Before you found me and Fuzz ball. That was bad enough."

"But I guess we're all trapped in cages really, especially the animals. The hollowed out living areas inside the asteroids are big and spacious, but they're not planets. There's not unlimited space that we can put aside for animals to just roam around in. It isn't like it's their natural habitat to live inside an asteroid, is it?" Torr pondered.

"It's not as if any of us can live in our normal environment. Sometimes I think about what it must have been like to live on Earth. I wonder what it would have been like to look up and see the sky above you. To see the real Sun up there above you without worrying whether you'd remembered to put your space suit on properly. The artificial sunlight they use inside the asteroids is nothing like the real thing."

The two of them looked at each other gloomily and sighed aloud. The mood stayed dark and despondent for a few moments with mutual depression before Fuzz ball pointed animatedly out of the window.

Outside, hanging motionless against the backdrop of stars and asteroids was the stranded space ship. The only way Torr could describe it was as a giant, red and white circus tent hanging in space.

A glittering, electronic sign that encircled the tent made a colourful, brash announcement, 'The Weird Circus of Dr Wonderfoul.'

"If they're so short of power, how can they waste so much on a sign?" said Nattie. There was a crackle on the radio. Someone was trying to communicate with them.

"Hello there, thank God you've come," came a voice they hadn't heard before.

"Dr Wonderfoul?" asked Torr, slightly uncertain who he was talking to.

"The very same. I'm so glad you've heard of me." There was a genuine, gooey, glee to the response.

Torr and Nattie just stared at each other in surprise. How could someone apparently stranded in space sound so happy about it? Nattie shrugged. She didn't have any explanation and the anomaly intrigued her.

"I wonder if you could be so kind as to help us," continued Dr Wonderfoul in the same sugar-laden tones. "We need a tow to the nearest centre of civilisation. For some reason all of our power batteries have failed at the same time. Dashed nuisance!"

Half of Torr just wanted to get on towards NördStrörm and whatever fate had in store for him. The other half was keen to take any opportunity to do exactly the opposite.

"We'd be glad to," he heard himself saying and Fuzz ball hugged his leg in excitement. She was clearly thrilled to be going to the circus, even a stranded one.

"That is indeed great news. Thank you, thank you, thank you. As a mark of our gratitude we'd like to welcome any of you to come over and visit our little circus of the weird and wonderful first hand."

The thought of going on board lifted the despondency and Nattie's face lit up. The possible plight of any animals the circus might have in captivity was momentarily forgotten along with the mystery of Dr Wonderfoul's odd reaction to his predicament. Fuzz ball bounced with excitement at the thought of what they might find aboard. Torr immediately knew that they'd be taking up the offer.

"That would be great," he said. "Thank you."

Even he felt a slight tickle of excitement. A few minutes later as they entered the airlock, Nattie tried to explain to Fuzz ball why she couldn't travel with them to the Circus. It wasn't going well and a disgruntled Fuzz ball shuffled off without waving them goodbye.

As the airlock door opened out into the blackness of space, Nattie looked at Torr who was eyeing her strangely. "I just don't know how to explain it to her. She thinks she's human and even though I don't know what she is, I know she's not human. They could have anything in that circus. What if one of their performing animals is another Fuzz ball? How would I explain that to her? She can't come with us until I've checked it out."

Torr shrugged and nodded. It seemed best not to say anything whilst Nattie struggled with conundrums, concepts and questions that he didn't have answers for.

Together they crossed to the 'circus tent' spaceship in silence. The main airlock was located just between the ticket booths. Inside a jolly looking, elderly man, dressed garishly in a flamboyant top hat and coat tails, awaited them. He greeted them warmly and enthusiastically, full of smiles and heavy handshakes. It had to be Dr Wonderfoul. Everything about him was over keen and slightly on the eccentric side of normal.

He had a long, waxed handle bar moustache that wriggled and writhed. It had small lights on each end that seemed to have lives of their own as they twirled and whirled with abandon. Nattie felt sure that the moustache was watching her as it gyrated erratically above the old man's lips.

The strange man's hat and coat were the oddest that Torr had ever seen. The colours never stayed the same, they continuously shifted around the rainbow; bright red, then deepest orange, followed by a gleaming canary yellow, cycling between each colour in turn. But the hat wasn't properly synchronised with the coat, so that when the coat was red, the hat was orange, and so on.

It was all very distracting and Nattie couldn't take her eyes off of the shifting, hypnotic patterns. The whole ensemble appeared to be trying to talk to her in a soft voice that she couldn't quite hear. But what was it saying? She couldn't be sure as a sudden weariness made her eyelids heavy. She tried shaking her head to clear it, but somehow her mind already felt too clouded and confused.

Dr Wonderfoul was bowing low before them, grinning wildly, swinging his flashing hat in a wide arc. His pyrotechnic display was having its usual emotional effect on these travellers. Their will power was already seeping away.

"I am enchanted to invite you to my circus of the weirdly unusual," he wheezed. "Please, won't you take a seat?"

With a flourish, he dramatically pulled aside a curtain to reveal the circus's central arena and a large array of seating. Inside there was total darkness except for a single spotlight on the centre of a sawdust ring, emphasising the shadows that surrounded it. Nearest to them they could just make out the back row of seating illuminated by the thin light it cast, but everything else was lost in the deep gloom. It didn't look very inviting but strangely and without hesitation Torr let Nattie go first and then followed obediently after her. Torr didn't even question why they were behaving so oddly.

It was only as they started to sit down that Torr realised that they were alone. Dr Wonderfoul hadn't followed them through the curtain and there didn't appear to be anyone else in the audience. Slightly unnerved, he tried to keep calm and sit casually in the large comfortable seats. Presumably something would start soon.

Suddenly there was a roar that shredded the silence, shaking off the stupor that had overcome them when they had first met Dr Wonderfoul. They both jumped in their seats. Nattie clutched at Torr's arm in fright whilst he tried to keep calm and think about it. This was a circus, which meant that there must be animals housed nearby, probably in cages. That was probably where the noise had emanated from. The two of them wouldn't be in any danger, would they? A circus would operate under all sorts of safety laws, or regulations, wouldn't it?

To calm himself he tried to figure out what was making the noise. Probably one of the big cats, a lion, or tiger, perhaps. But where was it? He couldn't see any bars between them and the arena, or more worryingly any lion tamer. What if someone had accidentally forgotten to lock one of the cage doors properly? He could feel his skin starting to crawl as tiny fingers of fear sneaked along his arms.

The roar came again, but closer this time. It didn't appear to be coming from the arena at all. Instead, whatever it was appeared to be making its way around the seating towards them. Torr's sense of unease escalated exponentially.

"Torr?" Nattie whispered, quivering next to him. "I think we should get out of here."

Torr nodded his agreement as another bellow rent the air. It was very close now.

Together Nattie and Torr backed towards where they guessed they had come through the curtain. Frantically, Torr ran his hands through the coarse, hanging material behind him, searching for the exit.

"I can't find the way out," he quaked as his voice was drowned out by another ground shuddering growl.

It was much throatier, almost on top of them. Something was infallibly heading straight towards them in the darkness.

"Here let me," said Nattie with almost a scream breaking through the thin covering of sanity that she'd hastily thrown over the primordial fear that now gripped her. "The way out must be there...somewhere!"

"It must be!!!!" she heard herself shriek uncontrollably.

Chapter 4: Kezin

Outside the securely locked tent flap, Dr Wonderfoul and three of his henchmen scrambled into their space suits. Each of the henchmen wore identical outfits; a metallic black construction encrusted with silver skull and crossbones emblazoned across the chest. Side by side, they all looked eerily similar to each other and you had to look carefully to notice any difference between them. Helpfully they had the numbers #1, #2, #3 printed on their backs.

Like his top hat and tails, Dr Wonderfoul's space suit and its striking insignia cycled through the colours of the rainbow. One moment the suit was red with an orange skull and yellow cross bones, the next it was yellow with a green skull and blue crossed bones motif.

And the hat? The hat was a hat to make the legendary Cat, jealous. Still firmly fixed to his head, the hat protruded through his transparent helmet like a skyscraper emerging from the smog.

Somehow, Wonderfoul managed to make the whole crazy outfit look as though it was seething with danger. All in all he appeared to be a sinister figure of bedlam, chaos and all round pandemonium, which is exactly what he was. Even the henchmen appeared nervous around him.

"Quickly men, we need to take over their ship before Kezin finishes his lunch," Dr Wonderfoul cackled inanely. "Once that wild beast has eaten those children he'll be much more docile and we can safely get him back in his cage."

From the inside of the tent came a terrifying scream. They all glanced at each other and grinned unpleasantly.

"Let's go," said one of the henchmen as he clamped his helmet shut with a click and a snap. "It looks like he's started."

Together they all moved quickly towards the airlock. #3 was at the front, followed by #1 and then #2.

Dr Wonderfoul sighed angrily and pushed his way between them, re-aligning them in numerical order.

"Incompetents!" he muttered.

~oOo~

Inside the tent, with mounting terror, Torr turned to face whatever it was that hunted them. Whilst he wasn't sure what he was going to do next, something inside him told him that facing what was coming was the right thing to do.

Destiny and fate smiled knowingly to one another.

Behind Torr, Nattie continued to frantically tug at the heavy canvas curtain in the vain hope that an opening would magically appear in front of them. She screamed at the unrelenting fabric in frustration.

In the darkness of the big top an ebony shadow loomed upwards from the ground, eclipsing the spotlight. Torr felt the air sucked into the huge jaws that opened in front of him before a hurricane roar almost knocked him backwards. He reeled before the onslaught.

Behind him Nattie switched on the flashlight attached to the helmet of her space suit, "I need to be able to see!" she squeaked from the edge of hysteria.

The fresh illumination gave Torr his first real look at the monster that confronted him. A shock of wild orange hair surrounded an almost, but not quite, noble face. All of the main lion features were there, eyes, nose, mouth, teeth (don't look at the teeth) but strangely elongated, halfway between those of cat and boy. The skin was covered with a soft downy fur that looked like it would be nice to stroke. But the teeth; the teeth were all ferocious cat and a very big, ferocious, cat at that. The lips curled in a snarl and Torr prepared for another onslaught of roaring that never came.

The lip uncurled with a note of cautious realisation.

"Hang on a sec. You're not Wonderfoul!" said the lion boy in a voice that was strangely pitched.

It was almost, but not exactly, an octave too high and given a serrated edge. Torr could only look back stupidly in reply. His entire vocabulary was frozen in fright. He didn't know what to say.

"What?" was the only word that came to hand.

No one had taught him what to do when you met a monster who mistook you for someone else.

Fortunately, the lion boy ignored Torr's lack of manners and pushed a large furry paw out towards him, "Sorry, if I scared you, I thought you were Dr Wonderfoul."

"Huh?"

Torr's brain was still running around in circles waving its arms in the air and screaming 'Mummy!', which wasn't much use and made it difficult to concentrate on sensible responses. But despite that he stuck out his own hand in return. The only rational thing to do seemed to be to ignore the total inanity of the situation and act as if nothing was wrong.

HEY! YOU'RE NOT WUNDERFOUL!!!

"I really hate him," the lion boy snarled, dripping saliva. "He has no concept that I'm anything but some ferocious beast and I'm not. No one deserves to be treated the way he treats me."

Half expecting the lion boy to play some trick on him and flay him with a single swipe of his giant claws, Torr watched his hand engulfed and felt the soft padding of a leathery paw. Unconsciously he scratched at his head, searching for the right thing to say to make up for his apparent lack of manners.

Fate giggled and Destiny sniggered.

"Well I guess that makes it OK then. I'm Torr and this is..."

Nattie emerged from the shadows behind Torr, switched off the flashlight on the helmet of her space suit and beamed a smile at the lion boy. Relief rearranged her features.

How come she knew just what to do? Why was it that girls always seemed to know how to react in awkward situations? thought Torr.

"Hi, I'm Nattie, do you mind if I stroke your fur. It looks so... um... furry."

Torr couldn't believe what she was saying and stared at her in some form of half shock. Was she mad?

"Sure. That would be nice. I don't get a lot of stroking," the lion boy answered to Torr's surprise. "Most people just run away when they see me," he purred. "There's a bit just between my shoulder blades that needs a really good scratch, do you think you could oblige? I'm Kezin by the way."

Nattie practically oozed herself up against the walking duvet of furriness that the ferocious cat boy had suddenly become. It was a good thing that Kezin was wearing a pair of shorts to protect his modesty.

"Wow, you sure feel nice, Kezin," she cooed, stretching out the last word into two long syllables. "Kezzzziiiinn."

Torr stared daggers at her. Moments ago she had been hysterical with fear and now she was all marshmallows and sentimentality. What was it with this girl? Was this normal? He didn't know. He didn't have many memories of his mother and there weren't many women that his Uncle socialised with for him to tell what was normal for girls.

"Hey, I don't suppose that you know a way out of here do you?" Torr asked, but no one appeared to be listening.

"Oooooh. That's good, right there. Oh wow!" purred Kezin.

The purring was in danger of getting out of control and didn't appear to have a volume switch.

"Well I know a way out of the ring, but that just leads back to my cage. It's usually locked but for some reason the door just opened itself about five minutes ago. That's what gave me the idea to get my own back on Dr Wonderfoul and when I caught your scent I just got mixed up. All of you monkey people look and smell the same to me."

"A cage! You have a cage?" gawked Nattie.

"I sure do," he announced proudly. "And I don't have to share it with anyone. Not since I ate the guinea pig girl..."

Nattie leapt off of Kezin as if she had been hit by an electric shock and instantly slithered behind Torr.

"You ate the guinea pig girl?" she whispered, peeking over Torr's protective shoulder.

Chapter 5: In the cage

"Of course not! What do you take me for?" Kezin exclaimed. "Just because I have these big teeth and claws people think I'm some form of beast," he looked like he was about to cry and sniffed loudly.

Torr wasn't sure that Kezin wasn't putting it all on for sympathy.

"I was about to say, not since I ate the guinea pig girl's supper," Kezin continued between loud sobs. "She was very upset and refused to perform for weeks."

Over his shoulder Torr could hear Nattie muttering, "Guinea pig girl?"

"Listen this is all very interesting," Torr interrupted, "but can you take us back to your cage? There might be something we can find there that will help us. If this exit is locked then it's likely that all of the other exits from the arena are locked too."

He was trying to make sensible headway against a strong counter current of confusion.

The longer they were out of sight of the Eos, the more worried he was becoming.

Kezin turned and started to weave his way through the seats.

"OK, this way," he called behind him.

Torr could still hear Nattie wondering out loud, "Guinea pig girl, lion boy, where are we? Whatever next, kangaroo kid?"

She couldn't help staring at Kezin's disappearing shadow and try to figure out what was going on. He walked upright like a boy, but he had the unmistakable movement of a cat. There was something about the way he shifted his weight from leg to leg, like his body flowed from one space to the next without moving through the air between. His walk had an underlying oddness about it. There was no hesitancy, or uncertainty in it. He didn't so much walk along as strut and swagger, with his long tail standing proud and upright, swinging hypnotically in time with the length of his stride.

"Torr, can you hear me?" came a whispering voice in Torr's ear. 'What now?' he thought.

"It's Kiki. There's some... erm... colourful people outside the airlock. They're claiming to be your friends. Shall I let them in?"

"No way!" Torr replied, now certain that they'd been led into a trap.

It had to be Dr Wonderfoul. How could he have been so stupid?

"OK, but they say they have a cutter with them and unless I let them in they're going to use it." Kiki paused as if trying to find the right words. "I think it might hurt."

"Alright. Stall them as long as you can," Torr replied, his worry about their space ship, Fuzz ball and Kiki, mounting rapidly. "We'll come and help out as soon as we can get there."

If anything were to happen to them...

But Torr had no idea how he was going to get to them, trapped as he was in a big top space ship with a lion boy and possibly a guinea pig girl. He did have his doubts though about whether there had ever been a guinea pig girl. It was all so unbelievable. Animals were animals and people were people, weren't they?

Kezin's cage was big and spacious. There was a large bed, a wardrobe and he even seemed to have 3DTV. There was a second exit into the main corridors but it was firmly locked. It had the unmistakable rumpled look of a boy's room; magazines were strewn around, clothes left where they fell and some used plates discarded casually. Further rubbish appeared to be shoved beneath the bed.

"So, what do you think monkey boy?" Kezin asked expansively.

"It's very, erm.., nice," Torr said lamely, trying to come to terms with being a 'monkey boy' and not wanting to upset the lethal looking lion boy.

"Well," interrupted Nattie, disappointed at not being asked for her opinion. "The monkey GIRL thinks it's lovely as well."

"You really think so?" Kezin looked genuinely surprised, turning to stare at her.

"I really do!" Nattie emphasised honestly.

Nattie and Kezin stared at each other for a few moments before she turned her head blushing and Kezin suddenly started tidying in the way that some boys do. For some strange reason he was suddenly finding extreme pleasure in steadying stacks of junk into neat and tidy, but unmistakably, unstable piles of rubbish.

Torr looked at the heavily locked exit before breaking the uncomfortable silence that had suddenly blossomed between Nattie and Kezin, "So all we need to figure out now is how to get out of here. Kiki, any ideas?"

There was a pause before there was a reply in Torr's ear, "I'm a little bit busy right now. But the cage will undoubtedly have some sort of fire escape mechanism." There was another pause. "It may not be obvious at first but there will be something to release you in the event of a fire."

"What's happening over there?" Torr asked anxiously. He'd momentarily forgotten about Dr Wonderfoul and his henchmen trying to break into the Eos.

"Too busy. Tell you later," and then there was only silence.

"Kiki?"

Nothing.

"Kiki?"

Torr's worry levels had now hit epic proportions.

Nattie came up and grabbed his arm. She could tell he was concerned, "Torr, what is it?"

"We have to get back quick. The Eos is in trouble. I suspect that Dr Wonderfoul is trying to steal it!"

"Fuzz ball!" wailed Nattie, cursing herself for leaving her cuddly friend behind.

"Come on, we need to start a fire," announced Torr, hoping that Kiki was right that there was a fire escape mechanism that would release them before they were incinerated.

"What! Are you crazy monkey boy? growled Kezin.

Torr ignored him, "Quick, let's get these magazines in a pile. If we can fool the automatic sensors it should open the locks to prevent us from getting hurt."

"Torr, do you know what you're doing?" Nattie asked aghast. "Isn't it dangerous to start fires indoors?"

"And so is being marooned in space with a hungry lion boy," whispered Torr as they stood over a small pile of magazines. "Stand back!"

Torr clicked the fingers of his space suit trying to remember how the Tinkerer had shown him to generate sparks from his fingertips. He hadn't paid much attention when he'd been told, assuming that Kiki would always be around to remind him. What was the point of having an electronic know-it-all if he wasn't there when you really needed him?

He tried again and miraculously a small spark leapt into life and disappeared into the pile they'd created. By chance he'd stumbled on the right combination.

They all waited expectantly to see if the fire would catch. Nothing.

Destiny gave fate a questioning look.

He tried again, still nothing. This wasn't working out in the way he'd wanted it to. He'd hoped it would be a lot easier to start a fire.

Soon they were all gathered closely; Torr and Nattie busily clicking their fingers to create sparks and Kezin holding the magazines bunched in his furry fists whilst blowing hopefully over every possibility of a flame.

"Got it," he shouted as the corner of one of the pages ignited. Piling it with the others they soon had a healthy fire going and smoke started to fill the room, drifting slowly between the bars that all remained resolutely in place.

"What if Kiki's wrong about the fire escape mechanism?" Nattie asked, clearly worried.

"What if we don't get back in time to save the Eos," Torr replied trying to see through the smoke that was billowing all around them, "and Fuzz ball!"

Nattie looked worried and Torr felt guilty. At that moment the sprinklers came on, showering them all in water. The fire went out a lot more easily than it had started.

"Oh that was so clever monkey boy!" said Kezin, who was clearly unhappy and dripping with fury filled sarcasm. "My nice, warm cage is now a soggy mess. It wasn't much but at least it was dry!"

Torr stared at Kezin in sinking dismay. The lion boy's thick fur was soggy and matted, clinging to his rippling muscles as his large chest rose and fell with anger. His whiskers drooped unhappily as the rest of him tensed, ready for a fight. Behind him he left a trail of wet footprints as he moved menacingly closer to Torr.

"All of you monkeys are the same! It's all a game to you isn't it. You just like to torment the rest of us. Well, when I get hold of you I'm going to do the same to you as I'm going to do to Wonderfoul when I get my hands on him."

His fingers made a wringing gesture that left Torr in no doubt about what was going to happen next. Monkey boy backed away from lion boy until he was up against the heavily locked, main doorway into the cage. With the wet hands of this space suit he pushed back as far as he could, his fingers unconsciously fumbling with the lock, slipping and clicking together.

Water and electricity never mix well. There was a crackling sound and the smell of burnt out wiring before the main door fell away behind him as he pressed against it. The way out into the rest of the ship was open.

Kezin's fierce face cracked into a grin, still full of very sharp and menacing teeth. "Well done monkey boy. Looks like your crazy plan worked after all and I didn't sacrifice all of my copies of Carnivorous World for nothing. Now, let's get moving so I can tear Dr Wonderfoul's head off."

ROBERT SMITHBURY
email: astro.saga.oblique.media@gmail.com

Chapter 6: Attack of the Overnight bag

Torr and Nattie grabbed their helmets, fastened them into place and cycled the air lock. Back in the locker room Kezin was ransacking the remaining suits trying to pull together something that would fit him.

"Kiki, hold on, we're coming!" Torr shouted into his microphone, hoping that someone was listening but there was still no reply.

He closed the inner air lock door with a grim look on his face. Kiki might be an annoying, electronic, know-it-all, but he was Torr's annoying, electronic, know-it-all. They didn't have time to wait for Kezin. Much as they were likely to need his assistance, the lion boy would have to follow along behind. He hadn't been happy about it but his thirst for revenge on Dr Wonderfoul was willing to make any sacrifice to get his paws on the circus master.

Torr and Nattie looked at each other anxiously. When the outside door of the air lock door opened, they stared across in awe of the open space between them and the Eos. It all looked quiet. Were they too late? Had Dr Wonderfoul already succeeded in capturing their space ship? Was it about to speed away from them, leaving them stranded? Torr couldn't see any big hole cut into the side. He looked around suspiciously, wondering if they were hiding somewhere nearby, behind one of the ships perhaps, waiting to force Torr and Nattie to help them gain an entrance.

Approaching the outer door of the Eos, Torr felt a lot happier when the doors eased open in front of them. Either Kiki was still in control of the ship's main functions, or it was an extremely elaborate trap. Torr's heart skipped a beat before the inner doors opened just as easily and they both stared in amazement at the scene that confronted them.

Henchman #3 was running around with the overnight bag jammed over his head. #2 was trying to fend off Kiki's tiny mobile unit which flitted around his head like a firefly. Meanwhile, #1 struggled to dislodge Fuzz ball who was clinging to his back like a limpet whilst ineffectively hitting him over the head with an empty box.

Amidst all of this confusion, the multicoloured Dr Wonderfoul stood defiantly at Kiki's main control panel frantically pushing random buttons.

He seemed to be unharmed but someone had battered his hat down, back inside his helmet and he didn't look particularly happy.

"Work, damn you!" he screamed petulantly slamming both fists down simultaneously.

There was a squeal and a squawk followed by the electronic equivalent of a burp.

Somehow, Dr Wonderfoul must have accidentally hit the right combination of buttons. Kiki let out the cybernetic equivalent of a scream and suddenly fell to the ground with a firm, conclusive-sounding thud. Immediately #2 leapt up and down on the fallen metal butterfly with destructive abandon. Sparks flew incoherently in all directions and there was a hint of ozone in the air.

Fate and destiny both looked at each other accusingly before glancing over their shoulders.

"Random chance?" asked Fate.

"Blind luck!" replied Destiny.

There was little doubt that Kiki was down. Nattie and Torr looked at each other for an instant before roaring out their anger and frustration. Together they leapt forwards to save what was left of their friends.

Disappointingly, Dr Wonderfoul almost ignored their joint war cry. With a wave of his hand he muttered, "Deal with them, I'm busy," before returning his attention to the control panel and the shifting pattern of lights. It was almost as if the computer's colourful display had some magnetic, kaleidoscopic attraction to the shifting colours of his own suit, dragging his attention inwards.

Torr cannonballed into #2, forcing him to give ground. The two of them struggled back and forth over Kiki's broken remains. Every crunch of splintered silicon and wiring beneath him made Torr wince in sympathy for his electronic companion. What if Kiki was somehow still able to feel what was happening as they ground his components into disembodied dust? It didn't bear thinking about.

On the other side of the cabin, the overnight bag made a sound like a vacuum cleaner launching into orbit. #3, whose head was still trapped between the zips screamed hideously. Grabbing both handles he looked like he was trying to wrench his own head from his shoulders as he grappled fruitlessly with the vicious, semi-sentient baggage.

Meanwhile, a struggling, captive, Nattie pummelled away at the chest of #1 with little effect. The uncaring henchman chuckled and only gripped her more tightly as Fuzz ball continued to cling to his back, the empty box discarded as it was proving to be pathetically useless.

From the speakers, a computerised voice gave out a low moan from far, far away, "Help me!" he cried plaintively as Dr Wonderfoul continued to punch the controls with sadistic emphasis.

There was no hint of Kiki's personality remaining in that pitiful cry and even that was fading rapidly. In response to Kiki's pleas Dr Wonderfoul just chuckled with the deep-throated gurgle that evil geniuses do.

The awful sound of that gruesome cackle appeared to revitalise the henchmen who renewed the ferocity of their attacks with sudden success. Nattie was thrown to the ground squealing loudly by #1 who shouted in triumph, catapulting Fuzz ball over his shoulder towards the air lock.

"No!" screamed Nattie as the ball shaped bundle of fluff sailed through the air, spinning gracefully, end over end, in the lowered gravity.

Milliseconds before Fuzz ball slammed into it, the airlock door opened. With a deft flourish, Kezin stepped into the room, dropped the bags he was carrying and safely caught Fuzz ball in his arms with a single movement.

The lion boy appeared to have had to make a painful compromise in his choice of space suits. He seemed to have found something that might have fit him when he was younger, but was now several years too small for his large frame. He looked uncomfortable in the yellow and pink stripes that had probably been designed for a clown with a penchant for pastels.

Fuzz ball looked up at Kezin as he held her close and threw her arms around his neck in gratitude. Her paws disappeared into his thick mane before he kindly lowered her to the safety of the floor behind him.

"You stay there," he growled gently, removed his helmet and pushed it along with his bags into a safe corner. He'd clearly decided to abandon his cage and take up residence elsewhere. It looked like Kezin had no intention of returning to the other space ship.

"I don't want my stuff getting damaged. Or anyone setting fire to it," he emphasised, glaring at Torr.

Turning with ferocity, Kezin gave a nerve-shredding and deafening roar. At the frightening sound #3 was panicked into successfully wrenching the overnight bag from his head. Underneath, what remained of his hair stuck out in porcupine style frenzy. Great chunks of it had been torn out by the roots, leaving large, red, painful, bald patches between. Turning his wounded head to check that his ears weren't deceiving him he stared open mouthed at Kezin, who advanced quickly with menacing teeth and claws. Dr Wonderfoul and his henchmen quickly huddled closely together as far as they could from the cross-bred carnivore.

What happened next was nothing.

Both sides nudged and feinted, moving first one way and then the next, trying to catch their opponent off guard, each carefully watching the other for an opening. But there was none. Kezin was between the invaders and the airlock and he wasn't going to take any chances. There was going to be no easy retreat for Dr Wonderfoul and his henchmen whilst Torr and his friends blocked their way.

"I've got you now Dr Wonderfoul," said Kezin and he licked his lips dramatically, deliberately giving everyone a toothy reminder of his dental hygiene.

Dr Wonderfoul didn't look as frightened as Torr had expected. He was terrified of the Lion boy and Kezin was on his side!

Dr Wonderfoul turned to his henchmen, "We know he's not as tough as he looks don't we?"

There were some nervous nods but they didn't look convinced. "He can't take all of us at the same time, can he?"

The nods were even less certain this time.

"Let's rush him!" shouted Wonderfoul.

And as one they did in some strange combination of manly bravado and idiotic loyalty mixed in with a large portion of uncoordinated line dancing. Although Torr did notice that the wary, wily, Dr Wonderfoul stayed slightly behind the others as they rushed towards the lion boy.

Kezin immediately disappeared under a wave of black space suits and initially it looked like Dr Wonderfoul had been right as they threatened to overwhelm the lion boy.

But first #1 was flung unconscious through the air where he would have collided with the airlock door if Nattie hadn't quickly opened it. #2, followed quickly behind, landing senseless on top of #1. On his own, #3 was no match for Kezin and he was quickly discarded with the others in the air lock.

Torr kicked their abandoned helmets towards them. He didn't want another air lock accident on his conscience.

Finally, there was only Dr Wonderfoul and Kezin staring at each across the cabin. Kezin glowered at Wonderfoul and Wonderfoul scowled at Kezin. Both appeared to be waiting for the other to move first.

Chapter 7: Dr Wonderfoul's last words

"Well?" Dr Wonderfoul paused before adding, "Animal!"

He clearly savoured the word, pouring derision into every slimy syllable.

Kezin growled menacingly low in his throat and foam flecked his fangs but Dr Wonderfoul didn't seem very worried.

"What are you going to do now?" hissed the sinister fiend. "You know I am your master. Now bow before me and I will let you keep your life. You miserable, pathetic, brainless creature!"

Nattie and Torr watched in astonishment at what was happening.

Torr had to admit to himself that Dr Wonderfoul had guts. He didn't think that he'd have had the courage to face an angry Kezin like Dr Wonderfoul was doing. And there was certainly no way that Torr would have deliberately goaded him further.

Kezin had descended deep into an inner frenzy of fierceness. His nose had creased up into a deep snarl, his nostrils flared, his whiskers winced and all of his teeth showed, nice and sharp, drooling with saliva. His muscles tensed and bunched as he crouched low, nearly lying on the floor, waiting to pounce.

Nattie's stomach curled up with the creeping tension, her muscles crawling under her skin. Irresistibly she peeked between her fingers, too fascinated to miss a moment.

Fate woke up Destiny who had drifted off to sleep. He thought she'd want to see this.

When it happened, it all happened quickly.

Kezin leapt at Dr Wonderfoul just as his suit was changing from violet to red. Maybe that had something to do with it. Astonishingly the leap never connected and Kezin landed on empty floor, his claws scrabbling for traction on the metallic surface. Dr Wonderfoul had vanished before Kezin had managed to grab him. Skidding to a halt, the lion boy gawked around him with a bewildered look of surprise and anger on his face.

"Over here, fool!" came a haughty challenge from the air lock. "I told you that Wonderfoul was your master as he is the master of every... beast!"

He almost spat out the last word and it appeared to hang there for a few moments, loaded with venom.

Nattie could see that Dr Wonderfoul was deliberately taunting Kezin, but why? Somehow the evil madman had managed to slip past the leaping lion boy at the last second. But surely he couldn't expect to keep up that trick forever? Eventually he must run out of room in the tight confines of their space ship. She couldn't understand what Dr Wonderfoul was trying to achieve until she noticed where his hands were resting. One was on the outer door switch for the air lock and the other was ready to close the helmet of his space suit. His henchmen had already pulled theirs back on. In an instant his whole plan became clear to her. Dr Wonderfoul was trying to trap Kezin in the airlock whilst he pumped all of the air out of it. If he leapt at Dr Wonderfoul now he would certainly die along with #1, #2 and #3.

Wonderfoul apparently had no regard for his underlings.

"Kezin, no!" she screamed as he pounced, deaf in his fury.

But Torr heard her and reacted instinctively.

If he had had time to think about it then he would never have thrown himself at the passing tail as Kezin hurtled by. Somehow he caught the twisting, twitching, writhing appendage as it whipped past, wrenching the vengeful lion boy to a halt in mid-air. If it hadn't been for the reduced gravity, he could never have done it, but Kezin's leap had landed short of its target.

When Dr Wonderfoul slammed the air lock door shut they were all still on the safe side with Dr Wonderfoul and his henchmen on the other. Torr had an instant idea and ignoring Kezin's regenerating fury he dived towards the control panel and used it to open the outer doors before ensuring they couldn't be over ridden from the interior of the airlock. With the door controls unresponsive, Dr Wonderfoul and his minions had no choice but to retreat back to their own ship, muttering curses and threats as they departed. For now the assault on the Eos was over.

Torr collapsed, finally feeling his quivering knees give way with nervous tension. It was all too much for him to take in. Being stalked by Kezin in the dark, starting the fire in the cage, fighting to recover the Eos, and witnessing the destruction of Kiki had all taken its toll on him.

Kiki! How would they survive without him?

Into the silence a familiar voice surprised them all.

"Well thank goodness that's all over," the mechanical marvel announced in a voice that dripped with false bravado wrapped in birthday-laden pleasantries.

A new mobile version popped out from a hidden access tray and hummed into the air in front of them.

"You're OK?" Torr said in total relief that Kiki was still alive and completely unaware that behind him Nattie was vainly struggling to restrain Kezin from ripping Torr's head off for daring to grab his tail.

She knew there was no way that she could physically stop him for long, so instead she stood on tiptoe and whispered soothingly into his pointed ears.

Gradually, Kezin started to calm down and retract his claws. Keeping Torr from Kezin's direct line of sight Nattie quietly led the lion boy gently towards the galley, before pouring him a bowl of cold milk. (Although Kezin was thinking more about a raw monkey steak than milk.)

"Of course I'm OK", Kiki was saying in reply to Torr's questions. "I was never in any danger."

"But you sounded like you were dying when you called out 'help me'."

"Oh that," Kiki said dismissively. "I was just play acting to lull that fiend into a false sense of security. He thought he knew my secret access codes but my engineering is way beyond anything he could ever hope to understand!"

"Humph!" said Torr disbelievingly. "Well at least that's all over now."

Relief flooded his wasted frame. He wasn't sure how much more excitement he could take.

"Maybe, maybe not," continued Kiki, "I have a message from.... Him!"

Kiki was clearly still rankled by the invasion of the Eos.

"Put it on," said Torr, wearily unable to argue anything more.

The speaker crackled with static as it struggled to keep a clear signal with minimal power.

"You won't get away with this. That... animal," Dr Wonderfoul almost spat out the word, "...belongs to me. He's mine, you hear! That's stolen property you have there. I'll have every policeman in space after you. I'll..."

Nattie switched the speaker off as she returned from the kitchen. "We've heard enough of that I think. You're with us now."

She put an arm around Kezin's shoulder as he drank his milk, eyeing Torr suspiciously.

HMMM! MILK....

"Thank you for coming to save us," purred Nattie.

"Yeah, what took you so long?" Torr asked, glaring back at the lion boy, glare for glare.

"I had to find a suit first and then I had to pack my things. I'm not stupid you know. I knew there'd be no time to pack later."

He fixed them with an intense stare.

"Don't ever think I'm stupid. I don't like it when people call me stupid," he emphasised and then gave the bowl a final lick that broke the tension between Kezin and Torr.

His large frame was still squeezed into the clown's psychedelic space suit with his thick, brown, bushy hair bursting out from every opening that the fight had rent in the fabric. Around his mouth the fur was now thickly smeared with milk, making him appear almost comical.

Torr and Nattie looked at each other and then burst out laughing with relief and after a moment's uncertain hesitation Kezin joined them, still not entirely sure why they were all laughing.

"I guess all you monkeys aren't bad," he muttered with an uncertain half smile. "You have nice milk for a start."

"You only think that because we haven't told you where we are going yet," Torr announced darkly, strangely feeling he was in some unannounced competition with the lion boy. "Ever hear of the Ice world? Us monkeys call it NördStrörm!"

The words tasted bitter on his lips. Every time he thought about their destination his mood darkened. He still wasn't looking forward to arriving.

Kezin didn't look particularly worried. "What's ice?" he asked. "Can you eat it, 'cause I'm starving. Has anyone got anything to eat? Milk's great but warm, red meat is better. I like it rare, very rare."

He bared his fangs in a wide yawn that showed his carnivorous teeth off to their best effect. Nattie, Torr and Fuzz ball all took a step backwards and looked at each other worryingly. Just how hungry was he? Hopefully they had enough food to keep him going until NördStrörm. None of them wanted to be trapped in close confinement with a hungry lion boy.

"What did I say?" asked Kezin.

~oOo~

For the next few days as they were all forced together in the close confinement of the Eos, Torr and his companions gradually became at ease with Kezin. The savage beast who had confronted Dr Wonderfoul had been transformed into an enormous kitten with just a modicum of care and affection. Lion boys, monkey girls and whatever Fuzz ball was descended from all took to relaxing on the sofas watching day time shows in those few hours when Kiki spared them the rationed power. Even Torr managed to tear himself away from his brooding about the threatening, approaching ice world to share in their brief moments of laughter.

Compared to recent events, the last stretch of space passed relatively quietly but once they were inside the asteroid conditions deteriorated quickly. NördStrörm had a different layout from Kingsley Downs. A large airlock positioned along the spin axis allowed space craft to navigate directly from space into the interior where most space ships navigated directly to the nearby space port at Vissenburg.

Kiki had planned for exactly the same thing but he hadn't reckoned on the blinding snowstorm that met the Eos the moment they emerged from the series of airlocks. It billowed and blew around their space ship, threatening to tear her from the frozen, storm swept sky as Kiki navigated towards the short distance to the spaceport. The whole interior of the asteroid appeared to be in the grip of a most savage winter.

The first thing they noticed was that the gravity wasn't operating at normal earth levels and was even lower than the reduced levels on board the Eos. They all needed to get used to even slight movements sending them flying across the room. Kiki had to explain the science to them slowly and carefully, several times.

"All space ships and asteroids generated gravity by spinning. The spinning acts like a playground roundabout, pushing everything that was inside, outwards, pressing people up against the inner surface of the asteroid, making them think of it as the ground."

It was this spinning to create artificial gravity that made docking without an ANP much more difficult and the main reason why the recovery of the First Celestial Secret had been so important. Now that the Second Celestial Secret was broken, everyone was trying to conserve power, NördStrörm more than others because it was further from the sun and less able to generate heat from its solar panels.

Reducing the asteroid's spin was one way to save valuable reserves of energy, but unfortunately it also meant that gravity was much weaker. This meant that on the inner surface of the asteroid everything weighed much less; fun for the children, but a severe strain for all adults. Whilst they laughed at the way Fuzz ball bounced playfully around the room pretending to be a balloon it wasn't long before Kiki bumped them back down with a harsh jolt of reality.

"Border control are asking permission to come on board?"

"It's OK Kiki, open up," Torr laughed in a rare moment of hilarity. "We don't have anything to hide."

He didn't notice Nattie sneak Kezin out of the door and into an interior corridor

Moments later, the air lock slid open to the frosty air of the spaceport and the two huge, waiting, men who came lumbering and grumbling into the room. They were dressed in thick furs and could have easily be mistaken for walking rugs, Torr thought, if it hadn't been for the long horns projecting from the top of their helmets. Even their heavy beards disappeared into the mass of knotted hair and tightly woven fabric, leaving two beady eyes peering out suspiciously from each grim and menacing face. Wearing a large array of spears, swords, axes and throwing knives clearly on display and ready for use, they were aggressively efficient from the start.

"Don't anybody move," announced the first, pointing at Torr with the business end of a very sharp looking spear. "You are all under arrest for smuggling."

ROBERT SMITHBURY
email: astro.saga.oblique.media@gmail.com

Chapter 8: It's not as if it's a tail

"We have reason to believe that there is stolen livestock on this ship," said the smaller and uglier of the two border guards.

"Yes," said the other, "animals, poultry, dinosaurs, that sort of thing."

Nattie quickly glanced around at Kezin. Dr Wonderfoul had obviously tipped off the border guards, who were probably going to search the ship. Where Nattie and Kezin were out of sight in the corridor they couldn't be seen but she realised anxiously that that was about to change. She had to thoroughly hide the lion boy quickly.

Quietly she led him further back into the ship. Somehow, she had to find a way to conceal him but it was going to be difficult to hide the large hulk of the nearly man-cat.

Back in the entrance lobby Torr was busy trying to stall the border guards. "Err, I don't think we have anything like that on board. There's just me … and my friend," he added, noticing that Fuzz ball was moving slowly closer to the border guards.

What was she going to do? Would they think that she was livestock? He had no idea and felt an unpleasant gulf of uncertainty open up ahead of him.

If Torr had known Fuzz ball better, he would have realised that she was only fascinated by the furry clothing that the border guards were wearing. Having cautiously sniffed their legs she decided that she just had to have a cuddle of their thick, shaggy, trousers. Lunging for one of the guard's legs she wrapped her arms completely around it.

"Fuzz ball, No!" said Torr. "Stop that!"

Torr leapt forward and started to pull Fuzz ball off of the guard's leg even as the guard started to reach for the axe hanging from his belt.

"It's OK," he begged, "she's just a pet. Please don't hurt her, we've got nothing to hide, honestly."

Torr gulped noisily as he realised what he'd just said. But it didn't look like the guard had put two and two together and realised that a pet was just another type of livestock.

For a moment he stared back at Torr as if there was something he was trying to remember. Shaking his head he idly swung the large axe in front of him.

"You don't mind if we look around then?" the guard asked sarcastically, replacing the axe and waving a hand held scanner around the room. "This will tell us if you have any livestock hidden anywhere. It can detect anything that's alive."

Torr wondered what it would make of Kiki. Was he alive? At times it seemed like he was.

With Fuzz ball struggling to get free from his arms Torr just nodded as the two bearded men pushed past him into the rest of the ship. He was beginning to panic. He'd already had one narrow escape and couldn't expect to keep that up that run of luck. It would only be a matter of time before they found Kezin and then they'd really be in trouble. He knew the ship was big after the Tinkerer's significant alterations and there were huge sections he hadn't even been in yet. But with a hand scanner, the border guards would find Kezin wherever Nattie was hiding him and when they did, what then? Even Kezin was unlikely to get past the heavily armed guards.

Torr needed to think of a plan, fast. He chewed his lip. Absolutely nothing came to him. Where was Nattie when he needed her?

Entering the sleeping area, Torr was as surprised as the border guards when they slid open one of the bedroom doors to find the room in almost complete darkness and Kezin tucked up in bed with the bed clothes pulled up to his chin.

Nattie sat at the side of the bed and looked up as they entered. "Oh! Hello?" she enquired sweetly, her hand coming up to cover her mouth as if she had just said something she shouldn't. "Please don't turn on the lights. My friend has felinitus and his eyes are very sensitive to light."

The border guards didn't know quite how to react and paused in the doorway, plunging the room into further shadow.

"Uh, hello," said one.

The other nudged him, "Go on ask 'em. He looks like the one we're looking for," the second guard said, peering into the gloom of the room.

His colleague still looked unsure. The darkness was unsettling him.

Kezin settled the matter by revealing one of his paws and waving at both of them inanely. Torr's heart sank.

"There you are, see, he has paws," declared the first guard.

"He does appear to resemble the description," muttered the second guard, turning to address Torr who was equally amazed at the scene facing them.

"Are you able to tell us a bit more about your... erm... pet, Sir?"

Before Torr could answer Nattie spoke for him, "He's not our pet. He's as human as you, or I."

Her eyes met Torr's, willing him to silence.

"If he's human then why does he have paws and a mane?" asked the guard suspiciously.

"The paws are a genetic deformity and a registered disability. It's a symptom of his felinitus, and that's not a mane, it's just hair and an unusual beard. I would have thought that two gentlemen with such wonderful beards yourself would be impressed by his rather splendid specimen."

The border guards turned to one another, both absent mindedly scratching at the hair cascading from their chins and peering into the darkness to discern which was the better beard.

"She's got a point. It is rather a fine beard."

"Yes, I might grow mine like that. Do you think a beard like that would look good on me?"

"Maybe, but I think it would suit me better. I have more hair on my head than you," answered the other.

The guards continued to argue amongst themselves for a few moments as Torr and Nattie exchanged meaningful glances. She pressed a finger up against her lips again to make sure he didn't interrupt her story and waited for the guards to finish their discussion.

The guards haggled between themselves for a few more moments before coming to a mutual decision.

"Well, whether he's a human or pet, he needs to come with us."

"And why's that?" asked Nattie imperiously. "What's your reason for arresting him?"

The border guard took a step backwards in surprise. He clearly hadn't expected any argument.

"We're not arresting him, Miss."

"Then, what are you doing? Confiscating him?"

"Erm..."

The two men spoke again. This time it was quieter as conversation continued in whispers between the two of them. There appeared to be a lot of confusion between them about what they were doing.

"Yes, we're confiscating him," they finally agreed.

"But you can't confiscate a person. It's not like he's property. He doesn't belong to anyone. Or is he a slave?" Nattie asked.

The border guards looked offended, "Certainly not!" they both insisted. "Slavery is against the law throughout NördStrörm."

"Well then, what's your reason for taking him? It's not as if he has a tail or anything!" she blurted out.

This started another round of arguing between the guards, more loudly this time, with lots of shouting and hands drifting towards their weapons. They didn't seem to have a clear idea of what to do with Kezin, or what he really was; human or animal.

Torr suddenly realised why Nattie had stayed seated on the bed the whole time. She was sitting on

Kezin's tail, holding it firmly down and tucked beneath the covers! If she hadn't, it would have been thrashing all over the place by now and given the game away. Whilst he'd seen lots of strange humans on his travels, he hadn't yet met anyone with a tail. It was such a give-away there was no way the guards could have ignored it.

A tail would make Kezin an animal and if he was an animal then he could belong to Dr Wonderfoul and be confiscated.

The two guards seemed to come to a conclusion. "OK. We'll let you go through however, keep a look out for someone looking like him, but with a tail. This animal appears to have escaped from some zoo, or circus, or something like that. He needs to be returned to his rightful owner. It's very dangerous and valuable apparently. There's a big reward out for it."

A very relieved Torr escorted them back to the airlock and they withdrew carefully through the doorway, bowing low to navigate all of their weapons through without accidentally amputating something. As the outer door closed behind them Torr raced back to the bedroom. Inside Nattie, Kezin and of course Fuzz ball were all laughing hysterically whilst slapping each other on the back with varying degrees of success.

"Enough of that," said Torr, interrupting the revelry. "That was fantastic. Such a clever idea to hide him in plain sight and fancy bluffing about Kezin's tail! Once you'd said that, there was no way they could ask anything else about it."

Nattie became uncharacteristically shy and her cheeks flushed scarlet.

"Yes, brilliant!" agreed Kezin. "I was worried when I saw Vikings."

"Oh they weren't real Vikings," Nattie giggled. "Real Vikings didn't have horns on their helmets. That's just a myth. I knew as soon as I saw the horns that they were all bluster and pretence. I guessed that just like all bullies with badges if we fought them with carefully thought through logic then they'd give way."

"What I don't understand," Torr muttered, "is why they were dressed up as Vikings, or pretend Vikings in the first place?"

"A lot of NördStrörm operates along Viking themes," Kiki replied. "It's common for each asteroid to have a differently themed environment. Early settlers had a lot of self-determination when it came to deciding local customs and laws. Some of them took it to unusual extremes. For instance, in NördStrörm, local building regulations require all municipal buildings to be constructed from organic materials. In the space port for example..."

"Enough already!" Torr interrupted wearily.

Nattie jumped off of the bed and Kezin's tail leapt straight upwards into the air, swishing wildly back and forth as if it had stored up all of his anxious momentum from the last few minutes.

"Come on!" she said. "We need to find that Aztex space ship. It has to be here in Vissenburg somewhere. This is the only spaceport on NördStrörm."

At the thought of tackling the Aztex soldiers again, Torr's heart sank. It had been bad enough in Kingsley Downs when they had somehow managed to recover the First Celestial Secret. They'd nearly been killed that time and their luck wouldn't hold out forever. Would it?

Chapter 9: Into the worst blizzard ~ ever!

With Kezin hastily covered up with several thick blankets, they emerged tentatively from the Eos. There was no sign of any immediate ambush and Torr relaxed slightly, taking a moment to take in the atmosphere of Vissenburg spaceport.

All spaceports looked different, reflecting the local cultural differences of each converted asteroid. Kingsley Downs had maintained a clear distinction between the spaceport and the asteroid's interior with gravity elevators providing the routes between the two environments. In Vissenburg the gravity elevators were inside the spaceport, operating as a conduit between the spacecraft parking bay and the spaceport's shopping centre.

The main interior of NördStrörm was sparsely populated, with open snow covered countryside and mountain ranges. The spaceport was, therefore, the logical place to locate the main trade and retail areas. But the vast shopping malls and eating zones were all deserted. Only a skeleton crew of security guards could be seen distantly patrolling the empty malls. Where were all the customers, wondered Nattie.

There was certainly a heavy emphasis on wood panelled interiors, thought Torr, reflecting that Kiki had been right about the Viking interiors. The dark stained timbers stretched in all directions, embossed with heavy metal-shod shields, spears, and hefty furs. Everywhere there were ominous signs of Vissenburg's flirtations with NördStrörm's Viking fantasies. Just how far had they taken this?

The uninhabited, shop-filled caverns of stained wood stretched out like spokes from the darker parking bays, located by the axis of spin. Here, long shadows hung like shrouds from the immense spacecraft that occupied them, cast by the bright lights that vainly attempted to illuminate the retail area.

At least the parking bays were busier with passengers and maintenance crew shifting around the overbearing bulks of their spaceships with unhurried purpose. They didn't appear to be in any rush to leave the axis and Torr wondered why.

More important to focus on immediately though was to find the Aztec spaceship and its impossibly valuable, secret cargo. He led the others in a methodical search of each parking bay and they found what they were looking for a short while later.

It was clearly a section of the Typhon. There was no mistaking the shape of a sphere, cut into eight equal pieces to escape the clutches of the Nebulon III. There was no other spaceship that Torr knew of that could do that.

Unfortunately, though, it was clearly abandoned. The main doors were open and there were scorch marks across the floor as if something extremely hot had recently been removed from the ship. Wherever the Second Celestial Secret was, it was no longer on-board. Reluctantly they turned about and headed back to the Eos.

Torr sighed and looked up at Kiki in exasperated expectation. The electronic marvel was fluttering above in his mobile form, flying this way and that as if he were a jellyfish with a sugar rush.

"What now?"

"Well I guess we turn on the portable tracker. Remember, the one that we talked about just before we ran into Dr Wonderfoul and his weird circus?"

Flitter, flit, flick, flicker, went Kiki, zipping backwards and forwards trying to establish triangulation points.

Torr could have kicked himself for having forgotten the portable tracker so quickly. "Yes, of course I meant that, I was asking if there was anything else I needed to know before we turned it on," he bluffed.

He felt foolish for forgetting something so important. How could the others depend on him if he kept making stupid mistakes?

"Nope!" replied Kiki, flittering around expectantly by the side of the Eos. "There's nothing more you need to know before we turn it on."

Torr pulled himself together. There was nothing more to do now. No more excuses to be made. It was time to face up to his future. A shiver slithered down his spine.

"Let's do it then," he said. "Where's the Second Celestial Secret been taken?"

Kiki turned in a full circle, "Hmmm, tricky, tricky, tricky. The huge double storm is hampering the sensors."

Around him they all stared, open mouthed, "Double storm?"

"Yes, double storm," answered Kiki. "The one we heard about on the way here has met another coming from the opposite direction. Now there's two of them causing four times the devastation."

That explains why no one is in a hurry to leave and there are no crowds in the shopping mall, thought Torr, ticking one mystery off of his long list.

Nattie turned to the nearest spaceport terminal window. Outside, snow was banked up in wide heaps and continued to fall heavily. The streets were eerily deserted as thunder rolled unfettered across the skies.

It certainly seemed that the Second Celestial Secret had been compromised. Here in NördStrörm, much further from the Sun than many of the other asteroids, the effects of the draining energy reserves were being felt much more quickly. If they didn't get the Second Celestial Secret back to the Tinkerer and fixed fast, then the whole of humanity had better get used to living in the deep freeze.

"Yes, a large double storm. The news channels are full of it. Something about it being the worst weather in memory, which is no surprise really. It's playing havoc with the sensors."

"Come on Kiki", Torr insisted. "Don't let us down now. If you can track the Second Celestial Secret as far as Vissenburg then you can find it in the middle of a mere double storm. This is Celestial technology we're talking about here. Surely the First Celestial Secret can help us find the Second. We have to go and recover it right now. We don't have any time to waste. We need to leave immediately. We simply must!"

Now that he'd made the decision to come to NördStrörm and recover the Second Celestial Secret Torr just wanted to get it over and done with. Youthful impatience seethed within him.

Nattie whirled around to face him. "Torr, you can't be thinking of going out in that storm! You won't survive it."

"But if I don't I might never find my parents again," said Torr.

Nattie folded her arms and glared at him, "Well if Kiki can't find it then there's no point in going out. Kiki I order you to stop looking!"

"I already have."

"Well done Kiki. I'm glad to hear that you agree with me," Nattie said, crossing her arms with triumphant emphasis.

"Oh I didn't stop because of what you said. I stopped because I found it," Kiki replied.

"Great! Where is it?" exclaimed Torr.

"The Second Celestial Secret is within a quadrant marked by the co-ordinates 34.22.36, 36.24.36, 34.24.34 and 36.22.36." Kiki replied emphatically.

Torr gave Kiki his best exasperated expression, "Go on surprise me, tell me something that might actually be useful?"

"It's located inside a building called The Tower of Neidelkreig. Your chances of successfully recovering all of the Celestial Secrets is less than 10%. 9.37519% to be precise," Kiki droned without emotion.

Torr swallowed hard. It wasn't quite what he was hoping to hear.

Nattie stepped into the gap, "How do we get there Kiki?"

"We leave the starport through the exit marked 'Way out to City Centre.'"

Symbols started to sweep across a holographic map that Kiki had helpfully started projecting into the air next to him. The friendly green line denoting their journey appeared fairly straight forward.

"…turn left at the end of the ramp and then continue straight on until we reach the Vissenburg expressway. Head spin-wise and follow on the expressway until you reach junction 7B, where we exit and head counter spin-wise into the …"

Torr had lost interest after the word 'exit.

"I'll get my snow gear on," he called over his shoulder.

He raced back along the route they'd taken from the Eos to the segment of the Typhon. Behind him Nattie stamped her foot and gave out a loud growl that Kezin would have been proud of. "Boys!"

~o0o~

Inside his cabin, Torr started to gather his snow gear. Item after item was thrust into the overnight bag, which somehow never appeared to fill up. Torr wasn't sure what the Tinkerer had done to it, but it sure made packing easy.

Before he'd finished, though, Nattie came into his cabin and tried once again to dissuade him once again.

"Torr, can't you at least wait until the storm is over, before you go out? It really does seem dangerous out there."

"Look outside, Nattie," Torr said, pulling on his snowsuit. "Kiki says the storm's not going anywhere and the snow is piling up rapidly. If we don't recover the Second Celestial Secret soon then the whole of humanity is going to freeze to death before we even get out of Vissenburg."

Torr was surprised that a complete calmness had descended over him compared to how frightened he'd been on the journey towards NördStrörm. Now that they had arrived he'd run out of choices. Ever since he'd won the argument with Nattie about going out into the storm his fear had strangely ebbed away, leaving a cold hard knot in his stomach. It was probably nothing, he thought and it was more likely that he was just hungry. Kezin had eaten nearly all of the food on board and they would need to visit the shopping malls soon to stock up. But right now he needed to get going.

Nattie was about to argue further when a noise from the doorway caught her attention. She turned to see Kezin and Fuzz ball standing in the doorway. They'd both dressed similarly to Torr for the cold weather and Kezin had remembered to keep his tail tucked tightly into his trousers.

Kezin spoke for both of them. "If there's nothing we can say to stop him leaving then the least we can do is go with him."

Nattie gave up with a loud sigh and headed for her room.

"Just wait for me to get ready, okay?" she shouted from the hallway.

There were still a few things she wanted to make sure that they took with them.

Despite his concerns about what NördStrörm held in store for them, now that he knew his friends were coming with him Torr felt better. He just hoped that he wouldn't regret it later.

If any of them had stayed to listen to the end of Kiki's route planning demonstration then they might have thought otherwise. The map now showed the friendly green line traversing mountainous terrain, zigging angrily back and forth across the landscape.

"...then take the footpath towards Mount Desperation straight in front of you. Keep to the left fork at 'Dead Man's avalanche' and travel through 'Killer Pass' until you reach the 'Glacier of Unbelievable Enormity'. Follow the glacier downstream until you reach the Crevasses of Cruelty, where the glacier descends over Valkyrie falls at the Tower of Neidelkreig. You will then have reached your destination."

Kiki switched back to his normal voice, "Of course, that would be under normal conditions. There are 17 severe weather warnings on route. Would you like to hear about those?"

He looked around him, realising for the first time that he was talking to himself.

"One of these days they'll realise that if they only listened to me..." he intoned unemotionally.

~oOo~

The snow was already whipping in their faces as they opened the doors marked 'Way out to City Centre'. They could hardly see where they were going. Within a few paces they were all head down into the driving wind that tore at every exposed piece of flesh. In the unrelenting gale Kiki was having difficulty hovering in one place and resembled an electronic parrot as he clung to Torr's shoulder in desperation in the tempest.

An hour later, after travelling only a short distance through Vissenburg they stopped again in the shelter of a large overhang from a boarded up shop. They were already nearly exhausted. Torr was beginning to realise that Nattie had probably been right. This was almost impossible. They hadn't found the Vissenburg expressway yet and meanwhile the streets around them were deserted and properties were boarded up against the weather.

Only Kezin appeared unaffected by their struggle with the weather. His wild mane rippled in the wild weather as he brushed at the towering wall of snow beside him.

"Hey, look at what we've got here," he announced.

He banged his paw against the large overhang and snow cascaded around them. "It's an abandoned snow sledge. If we can brush all of this off and get it moving then we could travel in style."

They all turned their frozen attention on the object that Kezin was beginning to dig free of the snow. It was a large platform sledge, capable of seating almost a dozen people in three rows of four. The back two rows had an all-weather cover that could be pulled down over them to create a semi-permanent shelter. Two enormous runners ran along the bottom providing an easy way of travelling over the snow rather than trudging through it as they had been for the last hour.

"And I guess you're going to push it all on your own, stupid," Torr muttered into the frozen wind as he jabbed at buttons on the dash board. "There's no energy to power the engine. The gravity might be a bit light but you'll never be able to move it on your own."

"Hey, don't call me stupid, monkey boy," Kezin bristled and bared his fangs.

Torr was too cold to notice, "Whatever. But you're not going to be able to push it on your own are you?"

"No, but..."

Nattie put a hand on both of their shoulders and raised her voice over their bickering and the screaming wind, "Stop it, both of you. Just give me a few moments. I might have a solution to how we get the snow sledge working."

She turned to Fuzz ball and knelt down, making strange hand signals in front of her. The small, round, furry creature shook her head violently and Nat waved her hands about again. With big eyes Fuzz ball looked up sadly at Kezin and Torr before waddling around to the far side of the overturned sledge.

"She looks upset. I'll go and speak to her," announced Kezin, but Nattie grabbed his arm.

"Leave her. She just needs a couple of moments of privacy."

All of a sudden, the ground trembled and chunks of snow scattered everywhere. A huge shadow loomed up over them and from the far side of the sledge a long hairy arm emerged from where Fuzzball had just disappeared.

"Look out," shouted Torr. "I don't know what it is, but whatever it is, it must have Fuzz ball."

Chapter 10: Breakfast?

Nattie grabbed Torr by the shoulders and screamed into his face so that he could hear her over the wailing wind.

"She doesn't <u>have</u> Fuzz ball. She <u>is</u> Fuzz ball."

Torr didn't understand.

"What do you mean, 'She is Fuzz ball'."

Behind him, Kezin took a step backwards, "Woah!" he mumbled, almost overawed, staring upwards.

The shadow swamped them and Torr looked skywards to see what Kezin was mesmerised by. It still looked vaguely like Fuzz ball, but a huge version, much longer and thinner overall, large enough to make Kezin look small and undernourished.

"How?" he whimpered weakly, the sight of a monster where Fuzz ball used to be was extremely unsettling.

"She's a transmorph," Nattie explained. "She can shift her shape between this form and the much cuddlier version. She just wants people to love her really, so she tends to stay in the smaller form rather than this one that sometimes frightens people. She doesn't like that. She never wants to upset anyone."

"I can understand that," muttered Kezin.

There was a growl from the Fuzz monster that seemed to support what Nattie was telling them. Torr found himself nodding furiously.

"But there are times when being this size is a lot more helpful, like now," Nattie continued. "Just try to remember that inside she's still the same shy, cuddly, little friend she's always been. Try and treat her the same way as you always have. Don't act frightened. It makes her angry and you really don't want to make her angry"

Torr gulped and tried to make sure that his head stayed on his shoulders as a large, furry paw tussled his head in what he hoped was a friendly, cuddly way. Probably just the way that Fuzz ball felt when he did exactly the same thing to her, he thought.

Another growl of assent and with an easy gesture Fuzz monster turned the sledge back the right way up again whilst shedding snow everywhere. She shrugged innocently while they quickly all bundled their belongings inside.

"I'll erm... give the lady a hand, I think." said Kezin and prepared to push alongside Fuzz monster.

Nattie and Torr just stared at one another in surprise for a moment at Kezin's behaviour before they both took up the load. Their muscles rippled beneath their fur as the sledge provided some initial resistance. Seconds later, after much grunting, they were under way again to the Tower of Neidelkreig, snow spraying up in a white cloud all around them.

"I may be able to help," announced Kiki, unexpectedly emerging from under the dashboard. "I've managed to divert some of the spaceport's power reserves to give the battery a bit of a charge. Now that Kezin and Fuzz …erm, Fuzz, have got us going it should have enough energy to keep us moving."

Torr smirked to himself. Was Kiki really struggling to figure out what they should call Fuzz ball just like the rest of them?

Kezin quickly leapt into the sleigh with the others. His exposed fur and clothes were caked in layers of ice and he looked like a walking snowman, but with value added; quivering whiskers and twitching ears. There were warm words of comfort for him as he leant on the edge of sledge and hauled a right-sized Fuzz ball back on board. Nattie hugged her frozen form close as the poor thing shivered uncontrollably.

As the sledge made its way deeper and deeper into the storm, the furry pair added welcome insulation. Torr pulled the cover of the sleigh down over them all and they snuggled together to gain what shared warmth they could in their darkly frozen surroundings.

He tried to make mental sense of his world as the howl of the wind outside drowned out any attempt at conversation. Everything he felt he knew for real was being turned on its head. His parents might still be alive, but the whole of humanity was in danger of extinction. Small furry, cuddly balls of fun were really giant, terrifying fur monsters and instead of staying indoors with a mug of hot chocolate he was urging his friends to head out into one of the most scary 'double' storms he had ever seen. And friends, since when had he had real friends? Travelling from asteroid to asteroid with his Uncle hadn't left much time for making friends.

But here they were, snuggled up against him, rushing onwards together into the great unknown. Whatever awaited him next?

~o0o~

Rapidly, they left the spaceport far behind them and headed off into the mountains. The snowstorm became worse, the scene reflecting old memories in Torr's head. Pictures of Christmas past surrounded by snow in all directions, mental images that he wiped away with a tiny tear that was wickedly snatched away by the wind as it dribbled shyly from his eye.

Unheard above the roar of the wind, Kiki continued to issue instructions about their direction as they carried on into the whiteness, leaving civilisation further and further behind. Finally, when their surroundings had deteriorated into a simple checkerboard of white snow and inky black sky, Kiki signalled a halt by shifting to flashing synchronised red and blue warning lights.

"We've come far enough. The Tower of Neidelkreig is nearby but it wouldn't be safe to get any closer before the morning. We should wait here for the dawn," he called out once the speed had dropped to a level at which they could hear each other.

Even Torr was too cold and tired to object.

"We're almost there," Kiki told them all. "We're on one side of a glaciated valley. The Tower of Neidelkreig, is on a huge, rocky outcrop beneath us but there's a large glacier between the Tower and us. In fact the glacier divides on either side of the rocky outcrop, practically isolating the Tower in the middle. It's a very treacherous geophysical manifestation of extreme meteorological and astero-tectonic conditions."

Torr listened as Kiki rambled on incomprehensibly.

"I don't think it's safe for us to try and cross to the Tower in the dark," Kiki continued. We should all try and get some sleep and see what things look like after sunrise."

That much Torr could understand and agree with. If he hadn't been so cold he would have half smiled at the thought of Kiki sleeping.

Outside, the wind howled long into what remained of the night.

~oOo~

The double storm blew itself out sometime before dawn and Torr was the first one to rise in the clear blue light of the morning. Nattie joined him a few moments later looking bleary eyed.

Together they stared out across the valley at the Tower of Neidelkreig. The tower itself was surrounded by a plethora of smaller, pastel painted towers that glittered and twinkled at them in the clear sunshine of a new morning, offering false hope and clarity. The cold air filled their lungs, sending traces of vapour into the air each time they exhaled whilst above them a solitary albatross wheeled across the

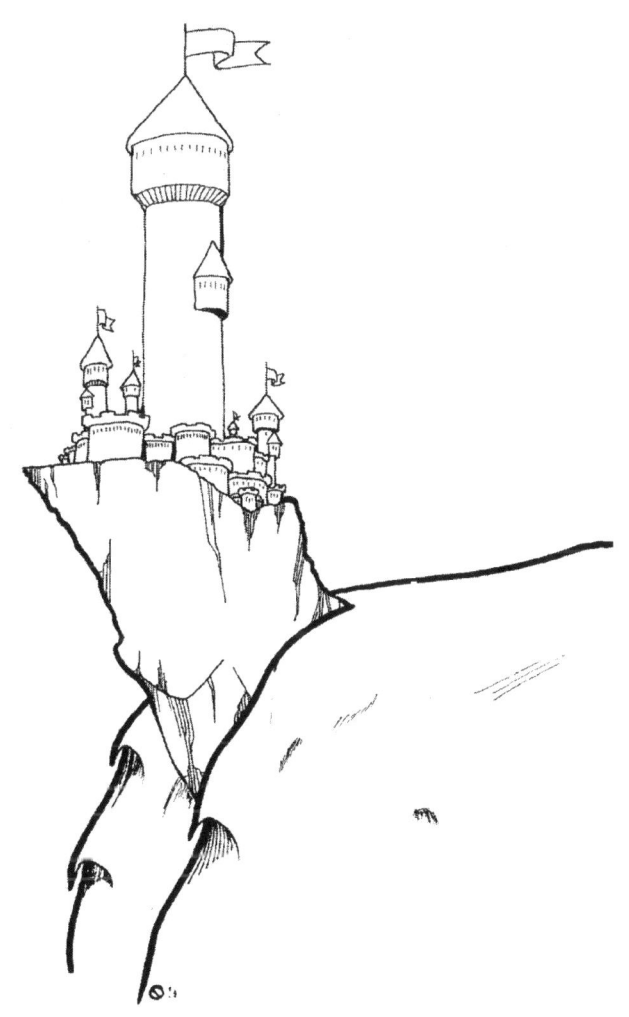

lonely sky.

"I'm not sure how we're going to do this, Nat."

She looked at him quizzically. "What do you mean?"

"Well, look at it. It's practically a castle. How are we going to get inside and get away with the Second Celestial Secret?"

The tower had been built on an outcrop of rock that dominated the surrounding landscape like a natural fortress. Someone obviously hadn't felt that was adequate and had further strengthened its position with tier upon tier of battlements that added additional, unnecessary fortifications to its already imposing facade. It cast a long, dark, ominous shadow across the frozen ice field.

On either side of the outcrop the frozen glacier split then plunged in two cascades of ice over the edge of a cliff. Before the extreme winter set in, when the glacier was still a wide flowing river, the tower must have been on the edge of one of the largest waterfalls in existence.

The frozen river provided no cover for a covert approach to the tower, which commanded views of all of the surrounding barren terrain. During daylight the occupants could see anyone approaching from far away. During darkness no one would be able to safely navigate the cracked and broken surface of the glacier. There was no way they could hope to get closer to the Tower without being observed.

Nattie took the map and with much glancing back and forth, compared it to the stark landscape. "This must be Valkyrie Falls. Goodness, it's huge. The map doesn't do it justice."

Crystals of ice clung to her hair as she paused for a moment. Her tummy grumbled loudly into the silence.

"Excuse me," she giggled. "Come on. Let's get some breakfast. I'm starving. We'll think a lot better when our tummies aren't nagging us."

"Breakfast?" said Torr uncertainly, sensing the big pit of ineptitude that was opening up in front of him.

Nattie looked at him hard, "Tell me you packed breakfast Torr, or at least some food. All of that stuff you pushed into the overnight bag. Didn't you think of putting any food in at all? You were the one who insisted that we all head off out here, so that makes this all your fault!"

"Well, erm, I was expecting us to find some shops or something," Torr whined, embarrassed by the weakness of his own excuse.

"Shops!" Nattie screamed at him, waving her arms around the vast expanse of snow. "And just where do you think these shops are hiding?"

She screwed the map up into a ball and threw it at him.

"Look, I'm sorry, okay?" He rummaged around in his pocket. "I have this one chocolate bar. We can split it four ways." Torr's stomach growled angrily at him as he pushed the chocolate towards her.

Nattie's stomach gurgled again as she smelt the sweet scent in the cold air. If it could have it would have reached out and wrenched the chocolate bar from his grasp before making a run for it.

Kezin climbed sleepily out of the sledge.

"At least I can let my tail hang out. There's not going to be anyone trying to confiscate me here."

He tugged his tail free from his trousers, stretched and looked around.

"Did someone say chocolate? I'm starving. I could eat anything."

He yawned and his sharp teeth glinted in the clear sunlight. The yawn turned into a low growl, which was smothered by his long, wet tongue that moistened his heavy lips. He stared at them blankly and expectantly.

Nattie snatched the chocolate bar from Torr's hand and quickly pushed it towards Kezin before her stomach shoved the whole thing into her mouth.

"Here you have it. We're not hungry," she lied easily at the sight of Kezin noisily devouring the bar.

"Yeah," added Torr wandering off in despair. "We're not hungry. Not at all!"

Some leader he was, he thought to himself glumly.

Around him the wind howled again as if to promise him that if there was a way that his life could be made more miserable then it would inevitably happen. Torr shivered, sadly. Well, at least he wouldn't have to worry about what the future held for long. In this inhospitable place they didn't have much of a future. They were likely to be frozen to the spot inside a few hours.

There was no point in trying to return, either. By the time they made it back to Vissenburg the whole asteroid would be too cold to be habitable. They might as well just huddle down together in the snow and prepare for the end. Torr stared deep into his own personal abyss of despondency and shed a tear of dejected, self-pity.

Chapter 11: The violent Verminx

Torr's self imposed solitude didn't last long before Nattie shattered it with a shriek.

"Torr! It's Fuzz ball. She's disappeared!"

"What do you mean she's disappeared? Here I am worrying about how to stop us sticking out like a sore thumb and you're telling me that a big, pink..." Torr struggled for the right words to describe Fuzz ball in her outlandishly bright snowsuit, "blob has just disappeared."

Nattie wasn't happy about Fuzz ball being called a blob, but she decided now wasn't the time to say. She was frantic with worry.

"Yes! That's exactly what I'm telling you."

Torr just stared at her for a few moments as his brain switched gears from self pity to rising panic.

"Missing? Then we'd better find her... and quickly, before the soldiers from the tower do."

It only took a few moments of running around shouting "Fuzz ball!" for them to exhaust all of the possible hiding places several times over and totally obscure any chance of following Fuzz ball's tracks.

When he realised what they'd done, Torr cursed his continued stupidity and tried to calm his frazzled nerves. He'd have more success using his head instead of his legs.

"Kiki? Do you have a heat sensor?"

Kiki nodded by bobbing up and down, his tentacles waving like long grass in the wind.

"Can you use it to spot Fuzz ball's heat signature?"

Kiki went silent for a few moments.

"Yes and if I can find her then I should be able to track a way through to her."

They all waited patiently, while fear and worry about Fuzz ball gnawed at their nerves.

Eventually Nattie couldn't hold back her trepidation any longer and spoke into the silence, "...and?"

"She's down here," called Kiki, speeding off down the slope towards the glacier.

They all followed at a run, slipping down the icy riverbank, sliding the overnight bag behind them. Close up, the glacier wasn't the smooth surface that it had appeared from the edge of the valley. It was riddled with fissures and gullies, the surface breaking and rising as the river of ice crawled down the hill at a pace that would have made a snail die of shame.

Fortunately, Kiki headed straight and true for a specific ravine hidden amongst the hundreds that littered the edges of the awesome glacier. He seemed certain of his destination.

The sides of the ravine were slick and smooth, with a constant stream of water sliding down the frozen surface that corkscrewed into a tunnel curving spin-wise into the interior of the glacier. Patches of illumination could be seen from light that fell and then reflected almost endlessly across the crystalline chambers awaiting below.

It was a natural water shute of epic proportions that any child would be hard pushed to resist. Clearly Fuzz ball had been beyond resistance.

Torr turned to the others, "Me first!"

He disappeared into the depths, closely followed by Kiki.

Kezin gripped the edges.

"If the monkey boy can do it then so can I."

Within seconds Nattie had been abandoned on the surface and the wild wind blew a sudden flurry of snow into her face. She drew back with a start and stared around at the empty wilderness that surrounded her. The shute suddenly appeared extremely inviting.

Inside, the steep sides towered above them, cutting the sunlight into beams of light and dark, creating patchwork shadows and starkly bright clearings. Their eyes adjusted to the constantly shifting light levels with difficulty.

Nattie pulled four head torches from out of her pocket and handed them around.

"I had a feeling that we might need these. It's like a maze down here. If it wasn't for Kiki I'd already be lost," she said. "And why is there all this water? Shouldn't it be frozen? It's certainly cold enough."

She shivered again, stepping over small streams of trickling water and trying to avoid the larger puddles.

Kiki started to explain. "There's friction at the edges where the glacial ice grinds against the rock, cutting out a valley. That makes heat. There's also pressure. The weight of all of this ice crushes the stuff at the bottom into water. The water wants to flow downstream faster than the ice and so rushes along through any gullies it can find, creating lubrication at the edges. We're lucky, this could be a torrent rather than a series of sedate streams. We ought to watch out for flash floods though."

Torr looked around at the myriad of crevices and side caves that Fuzz ball could have disappeared into. They seemed endless. It really was labyrinthine down here. He pulled on the head torch that Nattie had given him but he still couldn't see where Fuzz ball might have gone. The possibilities appeared endless.

"Kiki. Can you help here? What's the easiest way to get to Fuzz ball? If we aren't careful we could quickly get lost."

"Wait a second while I make a few adjustments. I'm going to re-calibrate the portable ANP tracker and route it through the astro-algorythm generator. If it can track a route through millions of floating objects in space then an ice maze should be no problem."

Kiki hummed an annoying tune to himself as circuits recalibrated and programs re-wrote themselves.

"Okay. Let's go left here, right at the next fork, then up, left again, left, right."

Nattie led the way and as they rushed along behind her, squeezing between jagged walls of ice, Torr was just thankful that they couldn't be seen from the tower. He stopped dead in his tracks as the thought seeped slowly into his brain.

Couldn't be seen from the tower? Brilliant!

"Kiki...."

But Kiki didn't hear him because at that moment they made the final right turn straight into a pack of wolf sized Verminx surrounding a petrified Fuzz ball. The small, vicious scavengers scampered and leapt about on their prominent rear legs, flailing tiny forearms in a frenzy of claws and teeth. Their bushy tails swept from side to side, creating a cyclonic blur of fur throughout the seething mass of carnivorous creatures that held Fuzz ball captive.

Fuzz ball had flattened herself against the wall of an ice cavern, whimpering pitifully. The pack that encircled her snarled and growled, oblivious to the arrival of her self styled rescuers.

"Do you think we can take them?" Nattie asked.

"I don't know. There's at least 30 of ..."

But Torr never finished what he was saying, because at that moment Kezin leapt past them and threw himself full length at the swarm of vermin. For a moment there was chaos and carnage as Kezin assaulted the vicious Verminx before they turned on him. He disappeared under a mountain of thrashing, howling fur. With blood flying in all directions, Fuzz ball ran squealing for Nattie, trying desperately to climb into her arms, weeping piteously.

Irrespective of how Torr might think of himself as a leader he certainly wasn't the sort who left his friends in the lurch. Taking a deep breath he threw himself into the melee, grabbing hold of the tiny, fierce, furry fighters and tearing them from the flailing, thrashing Kezin.

An out and out melee ensued and Torr almost fled when several of the Verminx converged on him. Their jaws snapped angrily at his face while he peeled others off of the lion boy by the scruff of their necks, their claws scratching at his clothes.

Holding a ball of whirling fury in each hand, he was trying to figure out what to do with them when a flash flood of freezing water caught everyone unawares. In seconds the trickling stream became knee deep before a sudden wall of water erupted into the cavern and broke against the struggling, frenzied fighters.

The Verminx scattered, yelping and squealing, wet fur matted and quickly freezing. Torr and his friends coughed and spluttered, as they were washed along, unable to fight free from the furious power of the flood, rushing maddeningly further into the maze of ice passages.

Chapter 12: Caverns of Ice

Nattie, Torr, Kezin and a bedraggled Fuzz ball were whisked away, desperately trying to keep their heads above the turgid, surging torrent. Kiki floated in the air above the maelstrom, whispering to the overnight bag that was happily bobbing away on the surface of the raging flood.

In the icy water Torr struggled vainly to make headway against the rushing tide. If they didn't manage to fight free then they'd be at the mercy of the current, heading at high speed into the unknown. Amidst the surging water he tried to force his brain to think. Where would all of this water be going? How could they escape from the desperate situation they were now in?

But it was a pointless exercise. A hissing, exploding sound dragged Torr's attention away from the impossible questions flooding his brain. Turning his head towards the source of the noise, he couldn't believe his eyes. The overnight bag was growing and expanding into a life raft. If Torr hadn't needed all of the air he could get he would have shouted in triumph and joy. The overnight bag had finally done something useful. Yes!

At the high point of Torr's elation, the flash flood washed them over a fissure in the floor of the ice cavern that was too slim for them to fall through. Only the water was pulled into a surging whirlpool that drained down through the hole, leaving them stranded and sliding across the icy riverbed.

The floodwater disappeared into the fissure with gurgle and a burp as it flushed away into the frozen depths of the glacier far below. The now useless life raft skidded about, joining the others on one side of the ice chamber in a futile pile of discarded flotsam.

Torr didn't care if the overnight life raft had appeared too late. He was just grateful to be alive. Struggling to stand up in his cold, wet clothing he brushed against the hairy rear wall of the tightly confined cavern they had been deposited in.

Nattie stared at him in alarm as he started to use the furry wall to try and dry his clothes against. With wide eyes she pointed at him, whilst trembling all over. Or not really pointing at him, Torr thought, but at something behind him. Was she pointing at something in the wall of fur, or at the wall of fur?

Wall of fur? What kind of a glacier had walls of fur?

Torr leapt sideways as a soggy Kezin sprung past him spraying a fountain of cold water drops in all directions.

"Leave this to me!" he shouted, launching himself at Torr's wall of fur.

The lion boy faced off against the hungry eyes of the hunter from the frozen wastes. As one, both the giant polar bear and Kezin bellowed their deafening battle cries at each other. Claws and teeth glistened in the shimmering light from assorted head torches that cast captivating shadows and haunted chimera across the frozen walls.

Between bestial roars Kezin shouted over his shoulder to his friends, "Run! I'll hold him back as long as I can."

The ice cavern reverberated loudly as the ponderous weight of the giant polar bear crashed back down onto its four legs It growled deeply and prepared to take on this strange contender.

Torr turned to Nattie, "We'd better do as he says."

His voice sounded shrill in the frosty air. Discovering that he had been rubbing himself dry on the great beast's furry coat had shocked Torr to his core. However, whilst he didn't like the idea of running away he wasn't going to be of much use to Kezin in this fight when all they represented was an extra target for him to try and defend. At least by continuing their quest they were giving him room to manoeuvre. It might just be possible, perhaps, for the lion boy to stay out of the beast's way until he could plan his own escape. Maybe.

The polar bear rose up onto its hind legs and towered over Kezin. The lion boy appeared small and insignificant by comparison.

"We can't leave him," Nattie cried.

She was close to tears.

"We have to. Fuzz ball needs us," Torr emphasised anxiously. "If we don't look after her, who will? We're almost her parents... we have responsibilities. We have to get her somewhere safe."

He knew he was gabbling. Even as the words were emerging from his mouth Torr could hear the shameful lie that he was trying to disguise with words of compassion. Deep inside, at an intuitive level, he knew that it wasn't Fuzz ball's safety that concerned him most. It was his own and that didn't feel right to him, as much as he tried to rationalise it, it just didn't feel right.

Fate frowned in consternation and Destiny hung its head in shame.

Nattie stared incomprehensibly at Fuzz ball who was clinging fearfully to her legs and shaking uncontrollably. Fuzz ball looked petrified. If Kezin thought he was going to get any help from the Fuzz monster it wasn't going to be any time soon. Nattie gathered the frightened creature up in her arms where she clung with an insistent and persistent tremble.

"Come on," shouted Torr, pulling at Nattie's shoulder and grabbing the edge of the rapidly deflating overnight life raft.

He started to run through the nearest open exit, hidden amidst the myriad of confusing walls and pillars of ice. He was totally lost and had no idea of which cave mouth they had come in through.

Nattie gave Kezin one last hopeless look of despair before she turned and headed after Torr. Fuzz ball still clung helplessly to her.

Even after they had turned a corner into a wider thoroughfare the noise of the growling beasts continued to reverberate around them. The pounding, crunching bite of their boots on the ice was fused into eerie echoes that pursued them as they fled. Running through darkened tunnels and illuminated only by the dimming light from their head torches, they squeezed between frozen walls that rumbled, crumbled and shifted around them. Unwittingly and unsuspectingly their thundering progress began to upset the delicate, internal slumber of the glacier.

Events are unsettling to glaciers, which normally have rather a sedate outlook on life. This one was no exception and Torr and Nattie fled unexpected traps and hidden dangers that appeared to pursue them. As they fled it felt to them that the glacier itself was attempting to devour them for their cowardice. Fissures suddenly yawned wide behind them, nipping at their heels, forcing their aching lungs to hurry faster. Ahead of them the ground would abruptly open wide, gaping over some bottomless chasm. Sudden and unexpected turns, reversals and diversions were all that prevented them from being swallowed by the voids that opened in front of them. Thinking became a forgotten luxury as safe sanctuary became the sole focus of every step and stumble.

Well, for the biological life forms it did, but Kiki appeared oblivious to what was happening around him. In total ignorance of the fear that gripped his shipmates he buzzed happily along beside them, providing a continuous drone of largely irrelevant information.

His words were wasted however, drifting straight through Torr's consciousness without encountering any sense of common comprehension.

"The last reported case of children being killed by a normal polar bear was in Norway, on old Earth, during 5th August 2011. The 'Evening Standard' for that day said that 'a boy was mauled to death when a polar bear attacked a group of students on a remote Norwegian island. Four other boys were seriously injured when the starving animal attacked the teenagers on Spitzbergen.' But that of course refers to normal polar bears before they were genetically mutated by the inhabitants of NördStrörm in their search for an enhanced Viking experience. The biogenetic engineers crossed the polar bears with sharks for ferocity, wildcats for tenacity, and the rhinoceros for size, demeanour and their ugly temperament giving rise to the hunter-killer polar bear... part of an eugenics breeding programme, now outlawed..."

"Enough already," wailed Nattie covering her ears as best she could whilst still fleeing mindlessly.

Kiki took the hint.

Gradually the distant sound of battle retreated without any sign of pursuit, allowing Torr's brain to finish the thought it had started way back when their most pressing problem had been finding Fuzz ball. But before he could speak, Nattie took the words right out of his mouth.

"Kiki, the whole glacier is like an underground maze. Are you able to use the ANP with the augmented thingie to find us a way to the Tower of Neidelkreig *through the inside of the glacier*? Down here inside the crevices we can't be seen from the tower! We should be able to sneak in unnoticed."

Torr abruptly snapped his jaw shut. Bother! That was exactly what he was about to say, but instead his hesitation had let Nattie grab the credit for the idea. Again! It was even more irritating that he'd known the right answer, he just hadn't said it in time.

"No problem. Turn left here," said Kiki, humming through the air, still blissfully unaware of the raft of human emotions that were running aground all around him.

The slim daylight was waning and the batteries that asthmatically powered their head torches were threatening a disappointingly early extinction when they finally came across what they were looking for. The icy walls unexpectedly parted ahead of them to reveal a sheer rock wall with what was clearly an airlock embedded within it. Futuristic and out of keeping with the heavily laden Viking overtures elsewhere across the rest of NördStrorm, the transparent double doorway reeked of a warm and much appreciated dose of modern civilisation.

The sight of it amidst the strengthening shadows gave Torr a welcome boost to his waning confidence that was nearly overladen with a nagging sense of guilt at leaving Kezin behind. He just hoped beyond hope that the lion boy survived.

Even if Torr hadn't been the last person to say it out loud, it had been his idea to get Kiki to integrate the two pieces of technology and here, even he could see that it had clearly worked. The only question left in his head had been how they were going to get into the tower once they'd found it. Well, here was the answer.

The engineers that constructed the tower had probably built its foundations deep into the core of the rock, he thought. But why had they thought it worthwhile to construct a modern and hygienic airlock into the rushing river that would have been here before the temperature fell? Unless they'd had some extremely powerful subterranean vessels that could fight the flowing river as it rushed towards the waterfall.

Standing in the deep puddles that surrounded the porch, Torr reached out to touch the plastic walls of the airlock. They felt warm, which was a welcome change for his frigid, frozen fingers. Another clue that the Second Celestial Secret was somewhere inside, he thought to himself. This place clearly still had power reserves that were denied to the rest of the asteroid.

Pressing his hands gently against the door, more to warm them than for any other reason, Torr felt the surface shift slightly. In the fading light he fumbled around for a handle, lever or lock. Warm metal slipped into his grip and it twisted as he turned it, opening inwards into a small, metallic chamber. They all slipped quickly inside and once the outer door was shut, Torr tried the inner one. That opened just as easily. A dark, damp corridor gaped wide before them.

In the stale air Torr glanced back at Nattie for reassurance before moving ahead into the darkness. Drawing on the power that seemed to saturate the air around them Kiki turned up his searchlight and bobbed along uncertainly ahead of them.

Torr struggled to make out any details of the tunnel ahead of them. A large net fell from the gloomy ceiling. Its weight dragged them down to the floor.

Torr had only moments to feel foolish before he was knocked unconscious by the blow from behind. Of course it had been a trap. Why else would the airlock have been so easy to open?

ROBERT SMITHBURY
email: astro.saga.oblique.media@gmail.com

Chapter 13: Hanging about... for a bit

Torr awoke but still felt like he was dreaming. Everything was woozy and appeared oddly distorted. His head hurt.

Looking around him through aching eyes, he could see that he was hanging above a large pit in a very dark room. From what he could perceive, ice gripped the walls in huge columns but it was difficult to tell from his upside down view of things. He was extremely cold and for some inexplicable reason only wearing his thin underwear.

Looking down he could see that the pit beneath him was far deeper than anything he had ever seen before. It almost appeared to be a tunnel leading downwards, disappearing into darkness, with what seemed to be a small circle of light far below, on the very edge of his perception. It twinkled so faintly that he wasn't entirely sure that it was even really there.

The only other dim source of light was from what appeared to be a hole, low down in one of the ice columns that encased the walls. Perhaps a way out, he wondered. If he could ever figure out how to untie himself and then survive the leap to the chamber's edge.

A blast of icy air swept upwards, suggesting to Torr that the bottom must open out over the frozen waterfall, which would also explain why the room was so cold. If the rope suspending him broke then the fall from here would surely kill him.

The realisation of the danger he faced staying where he was made him struggle to start thinking more clearly. He really was in a difficult position, in more ways than one.

Desperately, he tried to swing himself around so he could see more of the room. As he struggled to move the rope jumped and jerked him around spasmodically. He felt like he was a puppet at the end of an elastic string.

Twirling and twisting, he could see something lurking deep in the shadows by the wall; two burning red eyes that smouldered like twin coals and the sense of a figure hidden behind those eyes that was almost lost in the darkness. But there was something familiar about the way the figure crouched, close to what must have been a slim floor that hugged the wall. It was almost like a cat. A big cat.

Torr took a chance and called out quietly, almost whispering, "Kezin. Is that you?"

The figure shifted and slid forwards from the shadows, prowling furtively. It looked like it had once been Kezin. His formerly proud mane was ripped and shredded. Blood still ran from some of the thousands of tiny cuts that criss-crossed his fur. His eyes shone with a feral intensity blended with extreme fatigue. There didn't appear to be much human left in the strange mix of lion and boy. The fight with the polar bear seemed to have changed him almost beyond recognition. Would he remember that he had ordered Torr to escape, or would he only remember that Torr had run away, Torr wondered. Buried guilt brought a lump to his throat.

He tried to communicate again, trying to make himself understood by whatever humanity remained inside the wild beast in front of him.

"Kezin?" he asked again, softly, almost gently, pleadingly.

"Good to meet you again, monkey boy," the wild thing growled, smothering a full-blown roar and ending with something that was almost a whine. Or was it a yawn?

At least he was talking, but the words were slurred, difficult to understand, as if he couldn't be bothered to form them properly. Torr's mind raced, replaying what Kezin had said to make sure he understood what the almost unrecognisable creature was saying. Had Kezin said 'meet', or 'meat'?

Whilst Torr's mind whirled in confusion, Kezin crouched back down on the edge of the pit, muscles tensing.

Trying to work out when the last time was that he'd seen Kezin eat was making Torr's headache worse. It'd certainly been some time. Probably the chocolate bar, his stomach reminded him. That meant that Kezin must be extremely hungry and... and...

Torr gulped, trying not to think of guinea pig girl. Kezin's muscles were bunching and tensing; readying to leap.

He'd given Kezin the only chocolate bar for breakfast, Torr's grumbling stomach insisted again. Perhaps that might still mean something, but then he remembered that he hadn't given it to Kezin. Nattie had had to snatch it off of him. Nattie had given it to Kezin. Maybe Kezin thought that Torr had been hoarding it. Surely he wouldn't? Surely he would.

Torr resolved that if he survived then he'd be more generous in future, especially to hungry lion boys. IF he had a future, that is.

Kezin leapt forwards, a flash of feline frenzy, grabbing hold of Torr who started to swing at the end of the rope like a pendulum from the force of the impact. Talons gripped Torr's arms and he winced in pain. Swinging outwards in a wide arc, Kezin quickly climbed Torr's body, reached up and slashed with his claws at the rope that suspended them above the long drop over the frozen waterfall.

Before Torr could scream a warning the rope parted and their momentum carried them towards the edge of the pit. Torr couldn't see, but he was sure that they could never make it. It was too far, far too far.

Pitching Torr over his shoulder Kezin grasped for the edge, missed it and cat-like used his momentum to sprint up the sides of the pit. With a bound, spring and a wanton swagger they landed safely on the dungeon floor on the far side from where Kezin had started his leap.

Torr collapsed in a discarded pile while Kezin waltzed a few paces further as if he'd done nothing more than descend a steep staircase, his tail pointing up at a jaunty angle.

Torr didn't care. He hadn't been eaten and he was safe, well relatively. A huge swell of relief swept over him.

Despite all of his unuttered guilt at leaving Kezin alone to face the polar bear alone, the lion boy had come back to save him. Perhaps there was something on which they could build a mutual friendship. Surely saving his life had to count for something?

But whilst he might think he was safe and might even feel safe he was beginning to realise that had no reflection on reality. He was still trapped with a half feral lion boy in an ice bound dungeon, underneath a tower full of Aztex soldiers, wedged onto an outcrop of rock, overhanging a precipice, suspended over a frozen waterfall, inside a dying asteroid, millions of miles away from his parents and Uncle. He groaned out loud and life continued to slide inevitably downhill.

~oOo~

In the next dungeon along, Nattie was still hanging upside down from a long rope over a similar pit. But by the time that Kezin and Torr raced into the room she was already swinging herself across the room in a long arc, trying to free herself.

She screamed as they entered.

"Get out! Don't come in here!"

Kezin and Torr stared at each other perplexed and tried not to look at the swinging figure.

"Close your eyes. Someone has taken my clothes whilst I was unconscious. I've only got my underwear on. Don't look."

Torr, who had only recently recovered his own clothes, sniggered. Girls! He'd found his clothes, discarded with the overnight bag, in a corner of his dungeon, stashed there by someone, with the overnight bag discarded next to them. They were stiff with cold, but dry and they were better than running around in your underwear. For once he felt more composed than Nattie. There was something about clothes, or rather the lack of them that upset his sense of equilibrium.

"Shut your eyes before you come in!" she shouted again, as she swung past in another wide arc; her bare legs wriggling wildly.

Torr closed his eyes as Kezin yelled back, "If we have our eyes closed then how are we supposed to save you, monkey girl?"

Nattie swung back towards them again. "Use that nose, lion boy. It's big enough."

Kezin tried to stare at his own nose making his eyes cross.

"Do I have a big nose?" he asked Torr, who chuckled but kept his own eyes firmly closed.

Beside him Kezin growled aggressively in the dimness. Torr was about to suggest to Nattie that she shouldn't taunt Kezin in his current state, but before he could, he felt Kezin crouch and pounce, knocking him sideways with his tail as he flew past. Twisting blindly Torr's foot felt for a grip over nothingness and before he knew it he was tumbling into Nattie's pit.

His eyes snapped opened as he felt the floor disappear beneath him and the last thing he saw was Kezin and Nattie swinging to safety at the rapidly disappearing top of the pit.

Torr fell towards the darkness.

~o0o~

Elsewhere, Kiki floated silently, but swiftly through the maze of passages connecting the dungeons at the base of the fortress. He'd been left behind as a useless contraption by whoever had collected Torr and his friends. Ever since his automated systems had rebooted themselves he'd been searching for Torr, Nattie and Fuzz ball. But that was hours ago and the fortress was huge. Fortunately, it was also largely empty and he appeared to be the only one to have heard Kezin's roar. The lion boy was clearly still alive. At least for now.

If Kiki could find Kezin, he might also find the others.

Flying wildly into the dungeon he was just in time to see Kezin slash the rope that Nattie was suspended from.

Nattie spotted Kiki as she was propelled by Kezin towards the end of the arc of her swing,

"Save Torr!" she screeched.

Kiki stared around him, whirling in circles. He couldn't see Torr anywhere. Where was he?

Landing heavily on the far side with Kezin she gasped out the final piece of information that Kiki needed, "In the pit..."

Kiki accelerated to top speed and plunged downwards in pursuit of the falling Torr.

Chapter 14: Into the pit

With the arctic wind whistling past his ears, Torr realised that as quickly as the dim dungeon lighting disappeared from the top of the shaft it was being replaced by daylight coming up from below. At his present speed he felt sure that within moments he would shoot out into clear daylight with an unparalleled view of the frozen waterfall.

Not many people would ever experience that, he thought. It was a pity that it was likely to be a very brief spectacle, which he would only enjoy for a short period before he smashed into the glacier below. Torr dared not look down. He was too scared.

Suddenly, Kiki appeared, grabbed hold of Torr and tried vainly to reverse direction. His internal motors whirred frantically, trying to accommodate Torr's weight. His descent slowed marginally but not enough and where Kiki had hold of the thin synthetic fabric of his jacket it started to tear and separate. This wasn't going according to plan.

With his shirt shredding, Torr hauled the overnight bag from his back and clung to it desperately. Continuing to tumble end over end as they fell towards the glacier he shouted at Kiki and pushed the straps towards him, "Use this!"

Releasing the tatters of Torr's shirt, Kiki grabbed the other handle of the bag and tried again, pulling hard. The resulting stress unlocked the zip and the bag started to open. With dismay Torr noticed the contents start to unravel and open up around him. He could just imagine the embarrassment of the bag emptying all of his spare clothes right across the frozen waterfall. At least everyone would know which direction he'd been heading in before he hit ground zero, he supposed.

The overnight bag continued to unfold in mid air and an orange handle flipped into view, dangling and flapping in front of Torr's face. In friendly letters someone had stitched a message into the handle, 'In case of emergency pull, hard!'

It might be a parachute, or maybe not. For no more than a moment Torr considered his position. He was falling from a great height onto the jagged surface of a frozen glacier that was in the process of plummeting over a cliff. He hadn't eaten in nearly 24 hours, was half frozen and his clothes had been shredded by the only person who was trying to help him. If he pulled the handle could his situation get any worse?

Coming to the conclusion that even if it did he wouldn't have to worry about it for very long before the ground came up and hit him bone crunchingly hard, Torr jerked the emergency handle.

The overnight bag started to inflate. With feelings of regret and resignation Torr realised that it wasn't a parachute and the ground was only seconds away.

Tensing for the inevitable impact, Torr heard a scream echoing down from the tower before it was quickly stifled. Sadly he realised that no matter how bad his own personal situation was, he was still needed by his friends. With the ground rushing up towards him Torr realised that he was going to let them down in a big way again, one last and very final time.

The overnight bag engulfed him. Vainly Torr struggled to free himself, but before he could succeed the icy, frozen ground struck first. He bounced like a rag doll.

~o0o~

High above where Torr was making his mark on the landscape, Nattie had found her clothes and hurriedly struggled into them while Kezin rescued Fuzz ball from a similar dungeon. Moments later Nattie stared in disbelief as the two of them burst back through the doorway on the other side of the pit with two Aztex soldiers in apparent hot pursuit.

The first soldier was short, dressed all in black and hurrying regally despite his torn cloak. He looked far too short, almost a dwarf, she thought. But even as he rushed across the floor of the dungeon it was easy to see from the way he moved that he was used to giving orders and having them obeyed.

In his arms he clutched what she assumed was the Second Celestial Secret. It pulsed and glowed in a disconcerting way, as if there were some magical creature trapped inside, eager to escape. Its vivid light illuminated the dim dungeon.

The second soldier looked like a normal space marine. Only partially dressed in combat armour, he kept looking over his shoulder, apparently fleeing from some danger that was closing on him quickly from behind.

Nattie screamed and then stifled it quickly so that only a small squeak escaped around the edges of her fingers. She'd recognised one of the soldiers, the one in black. It was Lord Steal, the Aztex general in command of the Typhon where she'd been held captive.

"Lord Steal?" she gasped before he could say anything.

He turned at the sound of Nattie's voice, "So Natalia Vodianova, we meet again, though perhaps the circumstances could be more fortunate. However, as you are still alive there is yet a chance that all of my plans may nevertheless come to fruition! But not today it would seem."

His voice was a grating rasp; the sound of tin on gravel; breathless and devoid of emotion he glanced momentarily behind him. Then he stared back at her again, intently, as he retreated angrily across the dungeon with a look that impaled her with hostile blame.

The space marine behind Lord Steal didn't seem to have time to notice her. He was more interested in what was following close behind him as it exploded into the dungeon with a thundering animal howl of rage and anger. There was no longer any doubt that this was either a different, or the same giant hunter-killer polar bear, looking positively ravenous. The space marine seemed to be unarmed and was trying to fight it off with his bare hands as he fled. His space armour was being torn apart with battered, shattered and broken components strewn across the ground as he retreated vainly before the creatures relentless assault.

There was no doubt that his position was helpless. He was clearly overwhelmed and had very few options left to him. To fight was futile and yet abject surrender was unthinkable.

Nattie couldn't look and closed her eyes.

The soldier's struggles were worthless as Lord Steal, seeing the inevitable, deliberately shoved the soldier into the arms of the giant polar bear. It roared in triumph as it engulfed the space marine in its arms, hugging him as if he were some long lost friend.

The evil gambit gave Lord Steal the few moments he needed to execute his escape plan. With a desperate flourish he reached into a hidden pocket of his tattered cloak and revealed a …

… a teddy bear?

Lord Steal looked at it, surprised, confounded and annoyed. For an uncertain moment he raised it over his shoulder as if he was about to hurl it down into the pit. Instead, he pulled it towards him, gave it a quick hug and thrust it back into its hiding place before renewing his search of his pockets. Quickly, he found what he was looking for and pulled it out from its hiding place.

Torr gasped when he saw it.

A gun?

Was even Lord Steal careless enough to use a gun inside of the asteroid?

But before anyone could worry too much about just how careless Lord Steal could be, he surprised everyone once more. Instead of firing at the giant polar bear, or even threatening Nattie and her friends, Lord Steal turned and aimed high above the pit. From the end of the barrel a grappling hook snaked out and wrapped itself around the overhanging spar. With a tiny bound and holding firmly onto the other end of the rope attached to the grappling hook, Lord Steal leapt into the pit and started to lower himself down gently. In his other hand he still clutched the precious Second Celestial Secret, pulsating with flagrant energy.

Nattie couldn't help but be a little impressed by Lord Steal's marksmanship. He might be an evil warlord, he might be more than slightly annoying, he might even be a complete nuisance that just wouldn't go away, but there was no doubt that he was definitely a good shot.

He turned to face her again as he descended.

"I'm afraid that I must bid you farewell once more. This tower no longer suits my needs as it appears unable to access the power needed to hold back the glacier. I must therefore take this device with me and leave to seek greener pastures. Farewell, for now, for I hope we may yet meet again."

He waved a tiny hand and with those final words his head disappeared beneath the edge of the pit. Nattie was totally confused. What had he been gabbling about? But she didn't have time to ponder his words. She, Kezin and Fuzz ball were now left alone with the polar bear. The space marine's body was nowhere to be seen.

"Not again," muttered Kezin, darkly, as the bear advanced on them around the edge of the pit.

The bear roared, the tower groaned and chunks of the ceiling started to fall. The floor lurched like a trampoline.

"What's happening?" wailed Nattie. "Is this the end of everything?"

ROBERT SMITHBURY
email: astro.saga.oblique.media@gmail.com

Chapter 15: Waterfall wars

Down on the glacier, at the bottom of the waterfall, Torr managed to wriggle free of the overnight, all enveloping safety-cushion. Torr's on, off relationship with the ultimate travel companion appeared to have reached a new high. The combination of the lower gravity on NördStrörm and the padding afforded by the inflated bag appeared to have saved his life despite, or perhaps because of, the stomach churning bounce that had accompanied each impact. Glad for once that he hadn't eaten recently, Torr clambered out of the deflated remnants of the safety cushion that the bag had enveloped him in and looked around.

The snowfield directly beneath the pit was like a rubbish tip. That had also made a major contribution towards his soft landing. It was amazing what had been thrown into the pit over the years. There were huge piles of discarded 'stuff'.

Kiki tapped him on the shoulder with one of his connection tentacles. He turned around to see a large, discarded, Viking longboat looming over him. Its dragonhead prow staring down at him malevolently as if it was already aware of some future encounter they might have.

Even worse, standing at the stern, glaring at him intently, was the giant polar bear they had met earlier on the glacier. Vivid cuts scarred its snow-white fur with lines of unruly red. It growled aggressively, deep in its throat. There was little doubt it was the same one as it was still wearing some of Kezin's mane wedged between its teeth like some ornate ginger beard.

~oOo~

At the top of the pit, Kezin glanced from Nattie, to the hunter-killer, to Lord Steal's disappearing rope trick and back again in quick succession.

"Quick, this way!" he shouted before throwing himself headlong into the pit.

Nattie stared in disbelief. What was he doing? Had he gone mad?

The giant polar bear advanced ponderously towards her and Fuzz ball around the edge of the pit. Each footfall landed with a loud thud as the tower struggled in its ongoing fight to support itself. The weakening pillars continued to shake violently and a large section of the wall collapsed between her and the approaching beast. There was to be little respite as the enraged animal bellowed in frustration and started back around to come at her from the walkway on the other side of the pit.

There was no way out of it. The giant polar bear would get her if the tower didn't collapse on them first. Reluctantly she stared at where Kezin had disappeared into the depths of the pit. It appeared to be the only option left.

It was difficult to see what was happening in the gloom. Lord Steal had already descended about a quarter of the way but something seemed to have stopped him submerging further. He was desperately wriggling and flailing around at the end of the rope in an attempt to bypass the obstruction.

With a stiffed gasp, Nattie realised that Kezin was dangling from Lord Steal's boots, his claws sunk into the soft leather and fur. His leap must have taken him close enough to catch hold of the diminutive dictator as he swept past. Abruptly, with a savage kick Lord Steal crushed Kezin's paws and, with a howl of pain, the lion boy let go, falling with a look of foline surprise spread across his face.

Nattie didn't hesitate a moment longer. Lord Steal was going to pay for that.

Shouting "Hold on!" she grabbed Fuzz ball, who squeaked in shock and leapt towards the hanging rope. Climbing down it wasn't easy, but it was better than falling.

Behind her, major cracks opened up and more of the walls and ceiling started to collapse. With the deep, low, groan of a huge Goliath's death throws the Tower started its final fall with large slabs of rubble beginning to collapse into the pit.

Kezin's surprise at being dislodged from Lord Steal's foot was short lived. With catlike agility he twisted in mid air and prepared to land. Air streaming past him, he plummeted downwards, fur flowing behind him, arms and legs extended. Far below him he could see Torr running around and around the snowed in Viking longboat, hotly pursued by the other polar bear.

Realising that he had a chance of helping both Torr and himself at the same time, Kezin twisted once more, seeming to swim through the air as he fell. Extending his claws, he adjusted the final part of his fall, landing with arms and legs splayed out, squarely atop the polar bear. With a moan and a grunt it collapsed under the impact and lay there momentarily stunned.

His landing softened, Kezin leapt clear.

"Quick!" he shouted, grabbing Torr by the arm as he bounced off of the groaning bear. "Run!" he screamed.

"Not so fast," said a voice from behind them. "Stay right where you are. I have a laser gun and I'm not afraid to use it."

Kezin and Torr stopped in their tracks only a few feet away from the fallen bear and carefully turned to face the owner of the rasping, gravely voice.

Lord Steal released the motorised rope on which he had just descended, his short legs settling up to his knees in the snow. Both Kezin and Torr glared and stared down the barrel of his gun.

"Now, take me to your vehicle. I have an urgent need to get out of here. Without the Second Celestial Secret…" he brandished the large object in his arms, "…the tower won't last much longer. The failure of the Solergy batteries has plunged this asteroid into a new ice age. The glacier has been growing daily in power and strength, grinding away at the base of the tower until there's not enough rock left to hold it up."

There was a roaring sound from high above and dust started to fall around them like snowflakes.

"We don't have a vehicle," muttered Torr. The gun was making him nervous. "All we have is a 'borrowed' snow sledge. I'm not sure the battery has much charge left in it. We used a lot of it up getting here."

Lord Steal became angry and the laser gun twitched in his fingers. "Do you take me for a fool, boy?"

Removing his scarf to ensure Torr clearly understood what he was saying Lord Steal grinned horribly. Broken teeth gaped in a mouth surrounded by a heaving, writhing beard that wriggled like a thousand snakes. It seemed like every hair had an individual life of its own.

Lord Steal's voice grated on, "I will count to three. If you haven't told me where your escape vehicle is before then I will shoot your stupid pet."

"My pet?" gasped Torr.

His mind struggled to figure out who Lord Steal was referring to.

"Stupid! Pet!" exploded Kezin, clearly enraged at being described this way and preparing to attack.

His fur rippled and bristled. His lips pulled back sharply, exposing his fangs as he snarled.

Torr tensed. To attack would be suicide. Lord Steal would kill him as quickly as blinking. How could he stop Kezin? The lion boy had almost given his trying to save them.

Kezin's roar started off as a gravelling growl, a distant storm, soft and low in his throat. As the volume grew and his muscles tensed, it was quickly joined by another, almost an echo, faint at first, but rapidly growing in volume.

Lord Steal looked around wildly, trying to identify where the other roar was emerging from. Too late he thought of looking up, only to see the enormous polar bear from the dungeon plunging directly towards him. The lurching floors of the collapsing, crumbling tower must have thrown the beast into the pit.

With a worrying crunch, Lord Steal was plunged headfirst into the snowdrift beneath him by the impact of the polar bear landing on him from above. The laser gun and the Second Celestial Secret both rolled clear.

Overcoming his surprise in an instant, Kezin leapt for the gun. He sent snow scattering in all directions as he struggled to hold it in his large claws. But despite his best efforts he didn't have enough dexterity in his paws to grip it firmly and only succeeding in spinning the pistol high into the air.

The tip of his claw clipped the trigger of the twisting gun as it spiralled upwards. The laser beam burst into life, sending everyone diving for cover. From the end of the barrel an intense ray of scarlet light seared across the snowfield, scorching everything in its path. Angrily Kezin batted the laser gun as far away as he could.

Torr grabbed hold of an old piece of sailcloth from the rubbish surrounding him and carefully wrapped it around his hands before trying to pick up the Second Celestial Secret. It was sizzling softly as it sank into the deep snow. Despite the thick fabric, he could still feel the warmth of its power surging and pulsing inside its fragile shell as he picked it carefully up.

Somehow he'd managed to do it. He'd recovered the Second Celestial Secret. All he had to do now was get it back to the Tinkerer.

As if to remind him that this wasn't going to be easy, a large chunk of masonry landed in his footsteps with a muted thud. Looking upwards, Torr could see that deep at the bottom of the outcrop which the tower stood upon, a critical fault line in the stone finally fractured open. Above him the rock face cracked in two with a loud explosion. Unable to support the huge weight of the tower and overhanging cliff, the immense mass paused in shock before beginning a slow agonising slide down the frozen waterfall. An avalanche of ice, snow and masonry descended behind it.

From their perspective in the rubbish tip it looked like the sky was falling on their heads. The huge shadow of the crumbling tower swept across them and the thundering noise drowned out their screams. Amidst the tumult, the second giant polar bear, the one who had landed on Lord Steal, started to regain consciousness and looked around angrily. Trapped between two angry, hungry, giant polar bears and a mountainful of collapsing tower, Torr felt that he was destined to die here so close to success. Stranded on a frozen waste inside of a distant asteroid without ever seeing his parents or Uncle again, seemed like an unfair way to go, but there it was.

Destiny looked at Fate and shrugged disappointedly.

Chapter 16: It's in the bag...

With the tower collapsing above them Nattie and Fuzz ball landed in the snow, having carefully followed Lord Steal down his escape rope. Jumping the last drop as the line went slack from above, they joined Torr and Kezin who were preparing to meet the giant polar bears that were rapidly approaching them from opposite directions.

Chunks of rock rained down around them.

Seeing the inevitable danger, Fuzz ball stretched herself, her skin extending and expanding until she'd shape shifted into the unfamiliar form of the Fuzz monster once more. Even though the Fuzz monster dwarfed both of them, the giant polar bears continued to close in and she backed away in response. Large as she was, inside, the Fuzz monster was still only cute, friendly and very, very scared.

The two creatures continued to advance from both sides with bared fangs and sharp claws. But rather than tearing the four friends into shreds, they seemed more interested in each other than an early supper. Nattie watched in amazement as the bears rushed together and started nuzzling close to each other. It seemed that even bio genetically enhanced executioners need love.

"I think they like each other!" she shouted into the roar of the approaching avalanche.

But no one heard her above the groaning shriek of breaking rock.

The giant polar bears embraced as Torr signalled for everyone to climb aboard the Viking longboat. Inexplicably Kiki didn't follow and instead rocketed off at top speed across the frozen rubbish. Torr was surprised that Kiki could, or would, desert them but didn't have time to worry about the ultimate electronic companion whilst the tower started to rain down upon them more seriously.

Kiki would have to look after himself.

Kezin and Torr heaved and shoved the rear of the Viking longboat. They were both desperate to free the keel from the frozen ice and snow before it was crushed under the falling masonry. The ship refused to budge and all they succeeded in doing was to churn the snow beneath their feet into slush before falling into it face first.

Seeing that their efforts were in vain, the Fuzz monster gathered her fear and uncertainty into a lump of uncharacteristic conviction and jumped back out of the longboat. Sweeping them all up in her extended arms she threw Torr, the Second Celestial Secret and the overnight bag back into the boat before adding her strength to Kezin's.

There was a grinding noise that could be heard over the sound of the approaching avalanche as they struggled to release the keel of the boat. It juddered and jolted so much that Torr was worried that he might drop the Second Secret. Quickly he stuffed it into the overnight bag for safekeeping.

Torr wasn't convinced that the ageing timbers of the abandoned longboat could take the strain. Whilst it did, though, all of Kezin and Fuzz monster's strength seemed to be in vain as their feet skidded on the slippery, mushy surface.

At the last moment Kiki returned with Lord Steal's gun. With his tentacles wrapped around the grip he squeezed firmly on the trigger. A couple of well-placed shots from the laser pistol dissolved the ice, freeing the boat and it began to slide towards the edge of the frozen waterfall. The avalanche gathered pace behind it.

Clinging to the gunwales, Kezin and Fuzz monster quickly leapt aboard. With the boat picking up speed and miraculously staying seconds ahead of the falling tower, Nattie rushed to check that Fuzz monster was okay. The two of them hugged each other as hard as they dared to without breaking Nattie's ribs.

Out of the corner of her eye Nattie noticed that the giant polar bears had also managed to scramble aboard and were cowering in fear at the opposite end of the boat roaring in unusual trepidation and panic.

Above and behind them all, the sky split as the remaining supports in the tower exploded into oblivion with the strain of supporting the remnants. It made a sound like a thousand thunderstorms, eradicating any chance of speech.

The boat gathered momentum and as the Tower of Neidelkreig died behind it, it finally reached the edge of the frozen waterfall. Gaining momentum and an unhealthy dose of anticipated excitement it swept with inevitability down the incredibly steep slope that opened ahead of them towards the valleys leading to Vissenburg.

Everyone grabbed something to hold them steady. In a valiant attempt to influence their course,

Torr grabbed the tiller in order to steer the boat and signalled to Kezin to help him turn it. Kezin's tattered mane streaked in the icy wind as he added his strength to Torr's while the two of them struggled to steer a safer course. Kiki hooked onto Torr's shoulder and together they all slid over the lip of the ultimate, almost vertical, snow sleigh run.

Behind them huge chunks of the tower continued to crash into the ground with resounding blasts that set off a series of complimentary avalanches throughout the surrounding hills. Except for a small, clear avenue ahead a mountain of snow descended around them with all of the opaqueness of a thick autumn fog.

Amidst the deafening roar from the surging torrent of snow and rock, there were even a few howls of excitement. Surrounded by a growing sense of relief and elation their exhilarating ride seemed to go on forever, gathering more and more speed, until they could barely grasp the air to fill their lungs before it was snatched away from them. The icy air rushed past them as they fell further and further down the mountain and into the snowy valleys beyond.

With the welcoming lights of Vissenburg within sight and the slope levelling out, the longboat started to grind to a halt on the gravel soaked ice and snow that coated the lower slopes of the valleys leading down from the mountains. Even Fuzz ball felt it was safe to resume her 'normal' shape.

"Wow, what a ride," shouted Kezin over the wind, the boat now moving no faster than walking pace.

The keel began to grate more noisily underneath as Torr and Nattie started to exchange nervous looks about the two polar bears that were still sheltering at the other end of the boat. With the worst of the danger behind them they appeared to be gradually recovering their strength, bravery and ferocity.

"We'd better get ready to move quickly," Nattie suggested. "If we get off now then we can get a head start over those two great beasts. If we're lucky we might make it into town before they catch up with us."

Torr had to nod his agreement because he was lost for words. He felt totally drained, emotionally, physically and mentally. Gesturing wildly, they let Kezin know about their intentions.

He disagreed with angry gestures and indicated that they should ride it through to the end. He wore a stupid, lop-sided grin, with his long wet tongue hanging out, flapping in the breeze and spreading shaken saliva in all directions.

Torr shrugged, grabbed the overnight bag and jumped over the side. He had no strength left to argue. He tumbled end over end through the snow while Kiki hovered and fussed all about him.

Nattie dashed to the edge of the longboat, with Fuzz ball close behind, to check Torr was OK. He was already getting to his feet as unsteadily Nattie grabbed Fuzz ball and prepared to leap herself. Trusting in a soft landing and Torr's example she jumped clear of the longboat. The air swept them into the slipstream before ploughing them their own trenches in the freshly scattered drifts of snowfall.

Finding himself alone on the longboat with the two giant polar bears made Kezin give in to the inevitable. He wasn't keen to repeat his recent encounter with them.

With a swagger and leisurely leap he too jumped onto the edge of the guardrail with significantly more elegance and panache than the monkey people before him. Skilfully he balanced on the thin edge, judging his moment carefully and still grinning inanely, his tongue wagging wildly in the wind. Eventually he dropped to the ice with an easy grace, remaining upright as he did so with barely a break in his stride.

Clearly reluctant to return to normality, Kezin stashed his tongue securely back in his mouth again. The boat finally halted only a few paces further on, grounding on a gravely outcrop it wedged itself firmly into the rock with cracking creak, full of stubbornness and alacrity.

The four friends dusted themselves off in the echoing silence as the sounds of a new commotion began on the boat. Unexpectedly but with a decent amount of urgency, Lord Steal scrambled over the far side of the keel, hotly pursued by the two hunter-killers.

Somehow he had managed to sneak on board and remained hidden throughout the ride. Only now, when he had thought it was safe, was he attempting to make his escape.

He backed away from the longboat, the two bears following him cautiously, edging closer. Catching Torr's eye Lord Steal glared back at him and shook a diminutive fist.

"I never forget a face and I'll pay you back for this. Even if I have to pursue you beyond the Gates of Titan, I'll get back what's rightfully mine and have my revenge on you."

Torr was more amused than frightened

'The Gates of Titan', he pondered, wondering wherever they might be. It sounded like a tale from somewhere in his past. Something about alien invaders he remembered with gathering, mild excitement.

Sadly, Torr wished that circumstances might have turned out differently and given him a chance to discuss the Gates of Titan with Lord Steal. But that wasn't something Fate and Destiny were planning on him knowing any more about at the moment. Strangely, the diminutive dictator was more interested in talking his way out of trouble with two hungry bears than discussing the most important place in the solar system.

With a final backward glare and a grimace at the four friends, Lord Steal gave up any attempt at threats and negotiation as he started to run. The giant polar bears took one look at each other and picked up a pursuing pace behind him. The Aztex warlord's short legs frantically ploughed through the snow as the huge beasts lumbered more successfully and much more elegantly after him. Their heavy footfalls and low-level growls rumbled around the hills, threatening another avalanche. The last the four saw of Lord Steal was as he disappeared behind a snowdrift with the hunters only seconds behind him.

Chapter 17: ...or is it?

Much later, having slept and eaten at one of the recently re-opened hotels, Kezin, Torr, Nattie and Fuzz ball ambled across the departure hall of Vissenburg spaceport. The shops, restaurants and hotels had all re-opened. The cavernous space of stained wood and heraldry was awash with noise, light and colour, which was a welcome change compared to the endless white of the mountainous snowfield near Neidelkreig. The departure hall was full of visitors still trying to return home after being stranded by the earlier double storm.

It was strange seeing it so busy after previously having been so empty. Everywhere there were people, heavily dressed in furs, obscuring the steel arches of glass and metal. All wore their hair long and many had thick beards that almost obscured their faces. They all looked extremely fierce and wary. Most were still trailing a flurry of snow behind them, carrying heavy swords, axes and other sharp, largely unnecessary weapons alongside, what can only be described as, a selection of very ordinary luggage. Whole families appeared to be on the move, queueing for tickets, queueing for food, queueing for toilets, creating snaking obstacles everywhere.

Torr sighed. It seemed that wherever there were a lot of people there were going to be a lot of queues. He tried to lead his party through the throng and back to the Eos without losing anyone along the way. To his surprise he'd somehow got them all this far without misplacing anyone and he was keen to not let anything go wrong now.

Behind him Nattie and Kezin were deep in another argument about the relative merits of their different ancestry.

"Cats always land on their feet. That's why I didn't fall over in the snow when we left the longboat. Whilst you..." He moved his hands expansively, pretending to swim through the air. "...did a good impression of a snow plough."

"Rubbish," replied Nattie, clearly frustrated by Kezin's arrogance. "That was because the boat wasn't travelling as fast when..."

Torr smiled as their voices became a drone, merging with the hubbub of the departure lounge as he snaked his way through it. His smile suddenly disappeared when he thought he heard something he really wasn't expecting to hear again so soon.

"Two tickets to the Gates of Titan," said a voice from a figure lost far away in the crowd at the front of yet another queue.

"I'm sorry sir," came the reply. "We don't have any record of that destination."

Desperately Torr tried to see who it was that was buying the tickets but there were too many people in the way. Was it Lord Steal? Somewhere he had got the feeling that the Gates of Titan loomed large in his future but he couldn't explain why.

Before he could investigate further, however, the crowds of people quickly swept him away from the departure gate and any opportunity of finding out more.

He turned to Kiki who was still fortunately bobbing along beside him, "What's so special about the Gates of Titan?"

"Never heard of it," replied Kiki, much to Torr's surprise.

"But..."

"Think about it Torr, Titan's a large moon of Saturn. That makes it a long way from here. Saturn is a nearly 100 times further from the Sun than Earth. It's really, really cold there. There must be fewer than a hundred people who've ever even been there. No one lives there, let alone builds 'Gates'."

"But there was a man...."

"Noooo, no, no, no!" shouted Nattie, cutting across Kiki and Torr's conversation. "You can't do that. You can't leave us!"

"Hey, you're the ones leaving. I'm the one staying," said Kezin waggling his head, making his shaggy mane shake maniacally. "Monkey logic is just crazy."

"But you've got to come with us. We're..." Nattie hesitated, unsure of what she should say next.

"We're going to miss you," she mumbled

Nattie looked like she was going to cry and Kezin gave her that look that cats are so good at.

"But..." she mumbled, unusually unable to find the right words.

"No buts. This makes sense. Look around you. I fit in here."

Torr and Nattie took in the crowd of people milling around them at the furs and long beards, the sharp weapons and the wary looks. Nearby a sudden fight broke out over some minor bout of shoving near the back of a queue. Immediately axes flashed and fell, battle cries rang out, oaths and curses clashed and blood was spoilt before honour was satisfied.

Kezin laid a paw on each of their shoulders. "See what I mean? They think like I do. Fight first and ask questions if you survive."

Nattie nodded and then glanced down at Fuzz ball who looked distraught at all of the emotional upheaval around her. She stared up from face to face, fur rippling madly, unsure of who to go with and in that moment Nattie realised how much Fuzz ball really cared for Kezin.

Letting go of Nattie's hand Fuzz ball reached up to hug Kezin for long moments before releasing him and returning to Nattie's side. A tear ran into her face fur as she waved up at Kezin and even the lion boy managed to let go of his feline independence long enough to let a crooked grin wrinkle his lips.

Torr leant forward and grabbed Kezin's paw.

"You take care now, you hear?" he said, an unexpected lump rising in his throat.

The last twelve hours had taught him that lifelong friendships can be created in the strangest of places.

"You too, monkey boy. Don't go falling out of any tall trees now, or eating too many bananas."

He squeezed Torr's hand tightly and for a moment Torr felt that even if he had wanted to he wouldn't be able to tear his fingers away from the lion boy's tight grip.

"And just so you know, you did the right thing getting Nattie and Fuzz ball to safety while I tackled the polar bear back inside the glacier. I couldn't have kept all of you safe at the same time. It wouldn't have been pretty."

Torr could only nod with a lump in his throat.

"It looks like we both finally found our way out, I just didn't realise that I might actually miss you and your crazy monkey ways of thinking," Kezin said suddenly; he released his hand and wrinkled up his face.

Was that supposed to be a wink, wondered Torr, but Kezin had already turned away.

Even Kiki had a goodbye to say, nestling into Kezin's beard just long enough to whisper his parting words into the lion boy's mane. Nattie said nothing, but just waved. Together they all turned and walked up the steps back into the Eos, a heavy cloud of sadness above their heads. At the top of the steps she turned, but Kezin was already gone, disappearing into the crowd with a snarl and a swagger. She wondered if their paths would ever cross again.

"Let's go," she said. "There's nothing to keep us here and it won't be long before someone comes looking for us and the Second Celestial Secret."

"Five minutes to lift off," twittered Kiki, racing ahead of them with a whoosh of air and the intention of getting busy.

~oOo~

Behind them, Janx finally made it to the front of the long queue at the departure desk. Struggling to check in their scant belongings whilst keeping an eye on both

Jason and Sarah was stretching her caring mother's concern to near breaking point. Although at the moment, she had to admit to feeling a sense of relief that they were all still alive.

When the polar bear had chased the children across the frozen field she had feared the worst. Cowering beneath the bed for hours whilst the creature assaulted their cottage had convinced her that they were all about to die, but eventually it had apparently lost interest. Perhaps it had realised that the effort of digging them out wasn't worth it and had gone off looking for easier prey.

"Where to, Ma'am?" asked the absently courteous check in assistant.

"Somewhere warmer," Janx replied, glad to finally be leaving NördStrörm. "Somewhere I don't have to worry about polar bears coming around for dinner."

The assistant raised an eyebrow but when Janx didn't reply he continued searching the listings.

"How about Triassica? Tropical temperatures, abundant vegetation and even a theme park."

"Sounds great," replied Janx, not really listening, trying to catch sight of Jason and Sarah as they played 'it' across the busy departure lounge.

The departures assistant swiped her identity chip momentarily and then pressed the boarding cards into her hand. Without even looking at them she hurried to catch the children and get away from NördStrörm and its terrifying inhabitants as quickly as humanly possible.

~oOo~

Once the Eos had safely cleared NördStrörm and was coasting in clear space, Torr called the Tinkerer. When his old, friendly face appeared on the screen Torr couldn't help but notice that he seemed even older and more worried than the last time they had spoken. On the workbench behind him Torr could see half eaten sandwiches scattered around under scraps of discarded ideas, plans and dreams.

"So, did you get it?" the old man asked.

"Sure did," replied Torr, reaching for the overnight bag. "It's right in here."

He rummaged around inside the bag whilst the Tinkerer watched him from the large screen.

"Well?"

"I know it's in here somewhere. I remember putting it in here myself."

Torr's rummaging became more frantic. The Second Celestial Secret wasn't exactly small. His heart began to sink. How had he lost it? Had it rolled out? If he'd lost it...

Torr glanced up at Nattie who looked equally puzzled.

"Kiki?" Nattie asked. "Where's the Second Celestial Secret?"

"Why, it's in the bag," he answered.

Torr scowled at him.

"Isn't it?" asked Kiki innocently.

"You know full well that it isn't!" Torr exploded, getting angry, "Now where is it?"

"It was in the bag the last time I saw it," Kiki replied honestly. "Have you tried emptying it?"

Torr cleared a space at the table and upended the bag over it. All sorts of bits and pieces fell out that he didn't remember putting in there. There was an old rock, paper, scissors, string, a cheese sandwich, a Viking hand axe wrapped up in an old cloth, a compass, a blue pen knife with hundreds of blades, a pack of tissues, an empty drinks bottle and a bottle opener, just to mention the first few items that scattered across the table. But the Second Celestial Secret was conspicuous by its absence.

"Who put all this stuff in here?" shouted Torr.

He shook the bag violently, but nothing further came out.

"...and where did the Viking hand axe come from?"

"...and more importantly where is the Second Celestial Secret?"

ROBERT SMITHBURY
email: astro.saga.oblique.media@gmail.com

Chapter 18: The Mysterious Mystery of the Fish

"Perhaps I can help," suggested the Tinkerer gently. "Have you tried being nice to it?"

"What?" asked Torr, stopping in mid rant, his stamping foot still raised in mid air.

"Have you tried asking the bag to give you the Second Celestial Secret, nicely?" suggested the Tinkerer.

"What?" repeated Torr standing stunned, his mouth widely agape. He was so angry that he was unable to take in what the Tinkerer was telling him.

"Be nice to it if you want it to help you."

Torr gawked helplessly as Nattie gently removed the overnight bag from his frozen fingers. She cradled the bag in her arms and stroked the strong fabric.

"Please could we have the Second Celestial Secret back?"

The bag seemed to shrug in her arms.

"Perhaps if Torr apologised," the Tinkerer suggested.

"I'm not going to say sorry to a bag!" blurted out Torr before he noticed that Nattie was glaring at him. He reluctantly realised that they were all waiting for him to do something and sighed heavily.

"Huh, okay, look I'm sorry..." Nattie nodded at Torr encouraging him to continue.

"I'm, erm, sorry that I shook you," Torr felt foolish.

Nattie cuddled the overnight bag tenderly and it appeared to snuggle up to her. Torr couldn't make sense of what was happening. But then he never normally could make much sense of things that happened around the Tinkerer.

"It feels like there might be something inside."

"Well open it up and see," suggested the Tinkerer.

Sure enough, Nattie pushed her hands into the bag and pulled out the Second Celestial Secret, still wrapped in the large piece of old sailcloth from the Viking longboat.

"It's still warm," she mused. "As if it's alive."

"Pass it across to me please," asked the Tinkerer politely, but firmly.

Nattie placed the Second Celestial Secret into the Transportomatic. With one eye trying to watch the

Transportomatic and the other observing the minute screen to see what the Tinkerer was doing in the Eye in the Sky, Torr's eyeballs were in danger of crossing over one another. What he thought he saw was the Tinkerer opening a door he hadn't noticed before in the back of the Transportomatic, reach in and take out the Second Celestial Secret. But that wasn't possible. The Tinkerer was hundreds of thousands of miles away.

Torr scratched his head as his brain started to overheat from too much thinking about alien technology. Some things could only be thought about for so long before your mind started going around and around in circles.

He looked up and noticed that the Tinkerer was still talking as he worked on the Second Celestial Secret.

"...and I've upgraded the power potential on the Eos' engines. She should be able to outrun most human ships in space just as soon as I can get this power problem with the Second Celestial Secret sorted out."

He started tinkering with it.

There was that word again, said a voice in Torr's brain. 'Human'. Why did the Tinkerer have to say human, as if it was something different? Unless...

Stop it, stop it, stop it, thought Torr as his brain started circling uselessly again.

"There that seems to have done it! It was just a matter of re-calibrating the disabled fast Fourier transforms." the Tinkerer announced as the Second Celestial Secret started to glow brighter and brighter until it was almost too bright to look at.

He held the burning light in his hands pensively for a few moments as he looked for a place to stash it. "To think that all this is based on the calculations of the 18th century French mathematician Joseph Fourier. I'd better put this somewhere safe before someone else breaks it," he muttered almost to himself as he looked around his workshop for a spare space. It was in short supply.

Inside the Eos, Torr and Nattie grinned at each other as the lights grew brighter. The Second Celestial Secret was back in business.

Nattie laughed out loud, "I'd got so used to the low power that I'd almost forgotten how dim the lights were. It's good to be off of emergency power again."

Torr tugged at his jumper and started to pull it over his head, "And it'll be good to get out of all of this warm clothing."

He felt pleased that they had power back, and probably the rest of humanity was as well. "Kiki, you can turn the heating back on, now."

"I don't think I should turn it back on," said Kiki.

"Why ever not?"

"Well that will probably overload the life support systems. They've been on the blink ever since we got back on board. They're struggling to keep the air breathable and adding the heating won't help. Having the Solergy working again at full power is making things easier but it isn't advisable to take any chances."

Torr reluctantly pulled his jumper back on over his head. "Let me guess, this is something to do with the Third Celestial Secret."

"That's right," said the Tinkerer. "There's a delicate balance in any artificial environment, like a space ship, that needs careful monitoring and adjusting. Without it the air soon gets polluted and difficult to breath. Water needs purifying, waste needs recycling..."

"OK, I get the message," Torr sighed. "I need to get a move on and recover the Third Celestial Secret before people start dying from over pollution."

"Well, now that we've agreed that I expect you will want to get on your way," announced the Tinkerer with a smug grin on his face.

"Hang on a second," interrupted Torr indignantly. "What about my parents? Have you found them yet?"

The Tinkerer scratched at his head. "I've certainly made some progress. I know the direction they headed off in but no more at the moment. I've been very tired lately. I'm afraid that I've not been able to give it as much thought as I had wanted," he coughed. "I think it's the air. As the carbon dioxide builds up without the life support fully functioning it makes me feel sleepy."

He yawned and stretched.

"But I'll do my best."

He looked enormously tired, "I need to sleep." Reaching out, he touched a switch, "Good night," he said and the screen went blank.

Nattie and Torr looked at each other blankly.

"What now?" asked Torr.

"Visitors," announced Kiki.

"Visitors?" queried Nattie, looking quizzically at Torr.

They both rushed to look out of the window but were nudged aside by Fuzz ball who waddled up behind them and pushed her way through to the front. They all peered out into the blackness of space.

Torr stared in disbelief at a huge metal fish that appeared to be swimming alongside them; its fins and tail undulating gently as if there were some unseen current brushing them.

Who could it be?

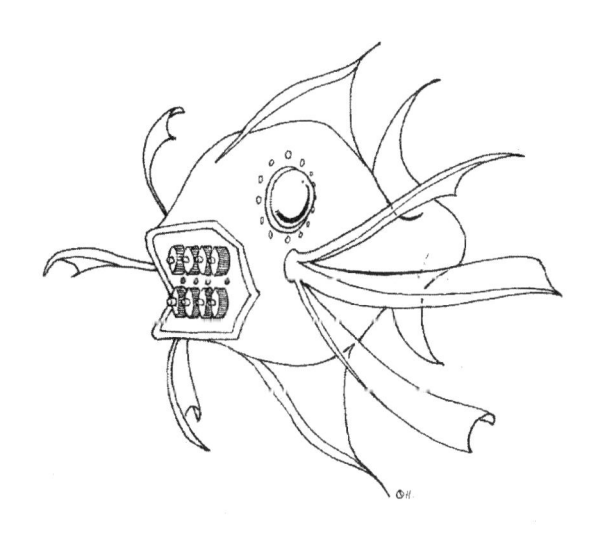

ROBERT SMITHBURY
email: astro.saga.oblique.media@gmail.com

Had Lord Steal caught up with them already? Was it Dr Wonderfoul, come to take his revenge?

Find out in *The Third Secret.*

The End of the Second Celestial Secret

I always love to hear what readers thought about my books so I can continue to write better ones. If you can leave a review where you purchased this, or drop me an email at

astro.saga.oblique.media@gmail.com

I would be really pleased to hear whatever you have to say.

Many thanks

Robert

Robert Smithbury

Printed in Great Britain
by Amazon

34542997R00121